Praise for
*Very Cold People*

"Though dealing with life's ugly, messy truths, her writing is compact and beautiful. So masterly is [Sarah] Manguso at making beauty of boring old daily pain . . . [the book is] a compendium of the insults of a deprived childhood: a thousand cuts exquisitely observed and survived. . . . This novel bordering on a novella punches above its weight."
                                    —*The New York Times*

"Manguso's attention to the chilliness and reservation of certain New Englanders crackles like a room-temperature beverage poured over ice. Manguso portrays the fears surrounding girlhood with a blistering clarity."
                                    —*The Washington Post*

"*Very Cold People* reminded me of *My Brilliant Friend*, the first novel in Elena Ferrante's Neapolitan quartet. . . . [Manguso] belongs to a cohort of minimalist, stream-of-consciousness writers—Jenny Offill, Sheila Heti, Eula Biss—whose texts work out the equations of domestic life and creative ambition."

—*The New Yorker*

"Chilling . . . This coming-of-age story offers a stark take on what it is to feel poor, poorly nurtured, and inadequately loved in a class-conscious, lily-white town. . . . *Very Cold People* does what we ask of good literature: It absorbs our attention and stirs empathy and reflection."

—*NPR*

"Reading Manguso is like watching someone skin an animal, slice its throat and drain its blood, preparing it quickly and efficiently for consumption. You wonder, reading her succinct and devastating sentences, just what she had to do to get there."

—*Los Angeles Times*

"In this carefully constructed novel, the pervasive cold is as human as it is meteorological. Manguso is an exquisitely astute writer."

—*The Boston Globe*

"Manguso is a lovely writer about unlovely things. . . .
A taut, blisteringly smart novel, both measured and rageful."
—*Kirkus Reviews* (starred review)

"Breathtakingly well-written."

—*Shelf Awareness*

"One of the most original and exciting writers working in
English today . . . Every word feels necessary, and she's re-
defining genre as she goes."

—JHUMPA LAHIRI,
Pulitzer Prize–winning author of *Interpreter of Maladies*

"*Very Cold People* knocked me to my knees. So precise, so
austere, so elegant, this story is devastatingly familiar to
those of us who know the loneliness of growing up in a
place of extreme emotional restraint."

—LAUREN GROFF,
*New York Times* bestselling author of *Matrix*

"A haunted masterpiece, written with the precision of a
miniaturist and the vulnerability of true heartache . . .
I wept more than once; I recognized myself more than
once. *Very Cold People* proves yet again that Manguso is
one of the greats."

—ANDREW SEAN GREER,
Pulitzer Prize–winning author of *Less*

"I loved every sentence, thought, and gesture in this perfect novel. Sarah Manguso has painted a deeply moving portrait of the stark unreality of childhood."

—CATHERINE LACEY, author of Pew

"A poignant and unnerving masterwork about growing up in a dominator society, told with the concision, carefulness, and sense of mystery that we've come to expect from Sarah Manguso."

—TAO LIN, author of Leave Society

*300 Arguments*

*Ongoingness*

*The Guardians*

*The Two Kinds of Decay*

*Hard to Admit and Harder to Escape*

*Siste Viator*

*The Captain Lands in Paradise*

Very Cold People

# Very Cold People

A NOVEL

## Sarah Manguso

HOGARTH | NEW YORK

2023 Hogarth Trade Paperback Edition

Copyright © 2022 by Sarah Manguso

Published in the United States by Hogarth, an imprint of Random House, a division of Penguin Random House LLC, New York.

HOGARTH is a trademark of the Random House Group Limited, and the H colophon is a trademark of Penguin Random House LLC.

Originally published in hardcover in the United States by Hogarth, an imprint of Random House, a division of Penguin Random House LLC, in 2022.

LIBRARY OF CONGRESS CATALOGING-IN-PUBLICATION DATA
Names: Manguso, Sarah, author.
Title: Very cold people: a novel / Sarah Manguso.
Description: First Edition. | New York: Hogarth, [2022]
Identifiers: LCCN 2021016059 (print) | LCCN 2021016060 (ebook) |
ISBN 9780593241240 (paperback) | ISBN 9780593241233 (ebook)
Classification: LCC PS3613.A54 V47 2022 (print) | LCC PS3613.A54
(ebook) | DDC 813/.6—dc23
LC record available at https://lccn.loc.gov/2021016059
LC ebook record available at https://lccn.loc.gov/2021016060

Printed in the United States of America on acid-free paper

randomhousebooks.com

2 4 6 8 9 7 5 3 1

Book design by Susan Turner

Very Cold People

1

My parents didn't belong in Waitsfield, but they moved there anyway. My mother answered the first knock at the door of the new house, expecting a casserole. *We'd painted the house Evening Fog,* she told me, *but the woman from across the street wanted to know why we'd painted it purple like Italians.* Some people wore their difference honestly, but my parents were liars, illegitimate Waitsfielders, their off-whiteness discovered only after the paint had dried. By the time I was born, the house had faded to the color of dirty snow.

The oldest houses in Waitsfield were older than the town and bore plaques to mark their age. Generations of families had been born and died in them, and the town's six graveyards were populated mostly by children. Over the centuries the slate stones had eroded and sunk in the dirt, and they looked like gray, crooked teeth inscribed with little lambs and angels.

On the way to school I walked past a three-hundred-year-old mustard-yellow saltbox that my mother admired for its leaded glass windows and historically correct paint color. It probably had all the right antique fixtures inside, big sooty hearths and Indian shutters, visible proof of connection to the first, best people.

My mother referred to western Massachusetts as *out west,* and I was mostly ignorant of the geography beyond our neighborhood. Three-quarters of the town stayed unknown to me, and that mystery drummed up a sense of scale. To this day I couldn't tell you how to get to the Lodge School, where the rich kids went. It was just there, somewhere, in those ten square miles, not for me to find.

I often asked my mother to drive us down to the part of town where every house had a plaque. It looked like a movie set. I knew a girl whose house had been used in a television ad for a clothing store. The ad was shot in the spring, and the crew had sprayed the lawn and the windowsills with sticky fake snow.

At home, my mother cut out wedding announcements from the *Courier,* the only paper in town. Maybe the groom was a Cabot, and the bride was an Emerson, and they sat on the boards of libraries and museums. My mother didn't know these people, but she liked the way they looked on our refrigerator.

She also liked to study an old typeset record of the town's census, turning the well-handled pages as one would a beloved picture book, but there were no pictures, just lists of names and addresses. She cross-referenced the addresses with real estate listings in the *Courier* each week. Sometimes she took me to look at the big old houses. I never saw any people, just the houses, big Georgian colonials with widow's walks and little gabled windows like third eyes opening.

I liked the estates, too, especially on Pond Road, which my mother told me was the most expensive street in town. Pond was a dead end, so it took some persuading to get my mother to drive the length of it and turn the car around, but when I reminded her that we'd never seen another soul walking or even driving around there, she could be tempted. Those houses weren't old. They were just enormous and ornate, with statuary and foreign-made cars. A couple of them were always under construction and hidden under blue tarps.

I recognized the difference between the houses that were the oldest and those that were merely the most expensive. I liked the old houses, and I swooned over the girls and boys at school with names like Verity and Cornelius. I knew that I could never build the kind of relationship with money that the people in those stately, drafty, oldest houses enjoyed. I didn't even bother trying to infiltrate them. I worshipped them from a distance.

———

In our house the old paint on the windowsill had its own sweet smell, different from the wall paint. I felt all around the window sash to find a draft, but there was none. The cold was just everywhere. After the monthly mortgage payment, my parents had almost nothing left over, and we had to be careful.

For one thing, the bathtub had to be filled to the height of my hand, and no higher. I pressed my fingertips into the bottom of the tub, not knowing where my hand ended and my wrist began.

One summer I found a green garden hose on the ground next to a neighbor's house. The hose had been left on. I tried to calculate the amount of water that had been wasted. *What are we gonna do?* I asked the other kids. They didn't answer. Adrenaline spilled into my blood. Water poured into the muddy ground.

An old Irish cable-knit cardigan with leather buttons hung in the downstairs coat closet, which smelled of hot farts and smoke. If anyone ever needed a sweater, they could go and put on the *warming sweater,* which was its name, as if other sweaters were merely decorative.

My mother kept the house just cold enough for me to need to wear the warming sweater over my regular sweater, and she cut just enough plastic wrap to cover the diameter of a dish.

I sat on the carpeted floor with my back against the radiator. It slowly bruised me, and if the heat came on, it turned my skin red in columns. A sheet of rigid plastic leaned between the radiator and the wall. It was meant to reflect heat back into the room.

Autumn brought with it the slap-clatter of crows, fire smells, leafy sweet-rot. New corduroys, cold air, brown paper grocery bags folded over schoolbooks. Writing on the first pages of notebooks, *September 7. September 8. September 9,* never sure how my handwriting should look.

We had two sugar maples in the backyard, and my mother liked them best because their leaves turned bright red, the furthest possible from their original green. One of the maples got sick, and she hired a man to cut it down. She said that the man had come and started cutting, and that she'd stopped watching him, and that when he came back to the house to get paid, she looked again and saw that he'd cut down both maples. Dead and gone. She would mourn those red trees the rest of her life.

When I walked home from school, I picked up leaves that were gold-specked crimson, green-edged vermilion, purple-black. I picked everything up, pebbles and matchbooks and little things people dropped. In December, I picked up evergreen branches and taped them to my bedroom door and made decorations, a little Christmas garland just for me.

One day my mother emptied my jacket pockets and found two half-used matchbooks and screamed at me. I could have started a fire. But I wouldn't have wasted a match to start a mere fire. I'd found what someone else had thought was trash, so I took it.

———

On winter mornings the light spread like a watery broth over the landscape.

My father drove a used silver sports car whose turn signals didn't work. Even in the winter, he stuck his arm out the window and signaled left or right as if he were pedaling a bicycle.

He started the car and let the motor run while I got into the passenger seat and wrapped the twisted black seatbelt around my lap. He scraped the windshields and the side windows with a beveled piece of clear plastic. I liked the sound of it, like a giant filing his nails. The bits of scraped-off ice looked like fluff; the air was too cold to melt it.

When my father got into the car with me he closed all the vents and turned up the heat to defrost the windshield. The car had spent all night drinking in the cold, and the cold in the car was worse than the cold outside.

After I said goodbye to my father and got out of the car in front of school, instead of continuing around the circular driveway, my father drove his little roadster down the hill and into the schoolyard. The little boys hooted and cheered. I watched my father pull the car back fast and do a three-point turn in the yard and then zoom back up the hill and down the driveway and into the street.

If enough snow fell, we had to navigate block-long ridges of snow between the roads and the sidewalks. Sometimes people walked in each other's tracks, and the one passable route froze into the snow in thigh-high holes.

One winter my mother backed her car into a pile of snow at the end of the driveway and couldn't drive it out. I called my friend and told her I couldn't visit her after all. She asked, slowly and gently, *Couldn't your mom ask a neighbor to help push it?*

But my parents never spoke to the neighbors; we might as well have lived miles from the nearest soul. It was too hard to explain why I couldn't break that silence, so I told my friend that no one else on our street was home.

On days that snow was forecast, we set our clock radios early to WBZ. If the snow started falling at just the right time and at the right rate, the plows wouldn't be able to clear the streets in time.

Public and parochial schools were announced in alphabetical order by district. *Abington. Acton. Andover.* When the announcer got to the *M*s I'd start listening hard, maybe close my eyes, because there was only one chance per half hour to hear it. Somewhere, someone was scraping at the snow with a metal shovel. *Uxbridge. Waitsfield. Wayland.* And then he'd keep going, as if Waitsfield meant nothing to him. *Wenham. Weston. Weymouth.* When he got to Woburn, that meant he was almost done.

If it was cold, the snow accumulated like dust. If it was warm, then the flakes melted together and fell in clumps. Sometimes school was canceled for snow that wound up melting by noon.

*One inch of rain equals ten inches of snow,* we all knew, but that had to be approximate, since there were so many different combinations of snow and ground.

I remember the metallic smell of it in the air before it fell. The pale blue of it on a clear morning. The soft *fuh* of it falling. The powder of the coldest days, too cold to melt, squeaking at the boot. White wet snow squeaking against my teeth, melting clear in the heat of my mouth.

Snowfalls have unique bouquets. Snow isn't just frozen water; it carries a remnant of the sky. A blue hailstone tastes
different from a white one because they've taken on air at
different altitudes.

We ate icicles not because they tasted good but because
they were a primal thing that could not be bought. To eat
one was to dare someone to tell you it wasn't clean, that
there was dirt in it, which we all knew; everyone eats a peck
of dirt in their life.

2

*Marry a man who loves you more than you love him,* said my great-grandmother to my grandmother, who obeyed.

And when that lady, my great-grandmother, got old, her children put her into a women's Orthodox Jewish nursing home. One day her eldest son visited and said he had something to tell her. And she said, *Oh—is it Abe?* It was. Her beloved husband had died. She had somehow known.

That was my family's great love story.

My earliest American ancestors got here at the end of the nineteenth century, not even a hundred years before I was born. It barely even counted as history. Real history was about Cabots and Lowells and Pilgrims and Indians.

After my mother's great-grandparents arrived from the old country, they were tailors in Boston, and their storefront had their name on it in gold. They had eleven children, and the youngest, my great-grandfather, ran the business into the ground. His sons grew up poor, but their cousins didn't. My mother said that my great-grandfather had had a lot of *lady friends*, and that was where the money had gone.

Still, my mother approved of these cousins and aunts and uncles I'd never met. Her uncle Roger, especially. He was an important man. And rich.

My mother hated Uncle Roger's wife, her aunt Rose. Why? *She had an operation on her stomach, and when Nana and I walked into her hospital room, she said to the people there, "And these are my poor relations."*

My mother clung to that story. She wasn't classy like Aunt Rose or Uncle Roger, but she wasn't poor enough to be called poor. I carefully remembered all the names and how sophisticated all of them were, in descending order.

Whenever we got together with the family, my mother claimed afterward that Aunt Rose had been mean to her. Uncle Roger was a big-headed Italian who had converted. My father was Italian, too, but he wasn't officially Jewish. He'd been prepared to convert, but he and my mother had had to take the class at the local temple together, and when he had outscored her on the test, my mother had said she didn't want to take the class anymore.

My mother's family all had wiry black hair and long, European noses. I envied their clannish sameness. I met my father's mother a few times, but I never knew anyone else on that side of the family because, my mother said, they didn't like Jews.

When I asked my mother why she hated her mother-in-law, my mother looked away and said, *She invited us over, and then a priest shows up.* Knowing nothing about Jewish history other than that Christians hated Jews, my mother cherished the injury of this priestly visit.

*Shalom means peace, and we love it so. We all say shalom for goodbye and hello.* Everyone else at Sunday school had a Hebrew name, but I didn't know if I had one, so I said mine was just Ruth, my regular name, which is a Hebrew name, so it sounded as if I knew what I was talking about. I named all my dolls Ruth, too. Naming them something else would have made my mother tease me. One day I asked one of my dolls what her real name was, and she said *Leona.*

Aunt Rose told me that her sister, my mother's mother, hadn't wanted to hold her babies and was sent to a home to get better, and that when she came back, she was never the same. And Aunt Rose told me that when he was little, her husband, Roger, had caught scarlet fever and had been sent to a sanitorium, and that his parents couldn't visit him.

We were once drying dishes at the sink after Rosh Hashanah, and there were others in the room, putting away wineglasses and silverware, stealing bits of cake from a plate. Aunt Rose was only half focused on me, on the chore, on her husband's mouth full of cake, on the way my mother had turned on the tap (too low). I thought of all the questions I wanted to ask Aunt Rose—what had happened to my grandmother? To Roger? To my mother? And what would happen to me?

———

One year my father handed my mother a dozen roses and said, *Happy birthday to the most unselfish person I have ever known.* It sounded like a sneer, but he often sounded that way, which anyone could tell if they called the house and got the answering machine. When it picked up, the cassette clicked on and then you'd hear my father saying, *You have reached—two three five—three one five five! No one is available—to take your call! Please leave—a message!* On the recording he sounded spitting mad. He probably was. He hated using machines. He was furious when they made him feel stupid.

My father wore a fake Rolex that ran about four hours before it stopped. *Get yourself a better watch!* my mother railed at him, and he said, with perfect hatred pinching at his eyes, *Better than a Rolex?*

Creditors called all day and into the evening. I had to pick up the phone and say that I was home alone.

My mother wrote *housewife* as her occupation when she filled out forms, but she spent a few hours a week sitting at the dining room table with photography trade magazines. She held a red grease pencil in her hand and turned the shiny pages, occasionally circling something or writing a number. When the crayon got too worn down, she pulled a little string and then unwrapped a long spiral of cream-colored paper, all around the pencil, down and around to its tip, and when the last bit of the paper pulled away, she had a spiral paper coil and a nice fat red crayon.

My father was an accountant, and he used his boss's old computer to type up reports for work. He couldn't figure out how to use the tab key, so he typed spaces between the characters and hoped they'd print as they appeared on the monitor, but they never did. Over and over, inserting and deleting individual spaces. The reports were a mess. I tried to show him how to draw a table, but he preferred staying mad.

*Just drag the disk image onto the trash can,* I called out, and he didn't believe me, thought it would cause the disk to disintegrate in the drive. *Get in here!* he screamed.

*Mother and the fourteen fuckers!* My father got artful in his rage. *Mother you fucking cunt!* My mother was more consistent. *Go shit in yuh hat!* she'd scream. *But he doesn't wear a hat!* I'd sometimes whimper. Years ago, the first time I'd said it, they'd laughed.

*My father never yelled at my mother,* my mother said proudly. *He only yelled at us.* My mother was two years old when her sister was born.

———

When we wanted to record a show, my mother looked in the newspaper's TV guide and noted how long the run time was, forty-eight minutes or twenty-two minutes, and programmed the VCR for exactly that long, not understanding that, with the ads, the shows ended on the hour or half hour. We never got to see the end. We all meekly accepted that this was the power the machine held over us.

In the tiny den, my parents and I sat and watched television. My father dabbed at his eyes sometimes, but my mother looked straight ahead, as if the television were just a rectangle of meaningless sparks. She might even ask if anyone was hungry, or sniff or sigh loudly, as if no one else were trying to listen to the show. My father seemed capable of being transported to Victorian London or outer space, but my mother was always just a woman sitting on an upholstered sofa in 1985. She was the protagonist of everything.

The three of us just about fit on the tiny sofa, though it was difficult because my father was always poking me in the side and my mother was always jiggling her feet, holding her hands between her thighs and twitching them, and making little sticky sounds with her mouth.

My mother got up from the sofa and sat in a wooden chair to the left of it, though I don't remember if the chair was always there; in memory it stands half in and half out of the doorway.

She sat in the chair and then slid herself down so her crotch pressed against the wooden edge of the seat. She gripped the arms of the chair and rubbed herself against the edge of it as if to scratch an itch. I held my breath. If I got up and left the room, I would be admitting that something was happening, in front of me, but if I stayed and ignored it, there was some small possibility that it wasn't happening, that it hadn't happened and never would. So I stayed.

And then my father looked at my mother. In that moment he seemed not to care that I could see his hatred on his face.

Meanwhile, I was reading all of the novels in the school library with the word *death* in the title. My mother taunted me about my *death books*, but I didn't stop reading them.

———

My mother's clothes were size large or extra large, but she only wore those sizes *for the length,* she said, and I believed her.

She drove me to Calvert's to buy factory seconds for my school clothes. Knit polyester turtlenecks were twenty-nine cents apiece, and I got seven of them. One was white as paint. One had little red hearts on it in rows. Another was a toxic pink. One day in art class another girl proposed that we go around the table and say something that we didn't like about someone else at the table. She let someone else go first. Then, when it was her turn, she said, *I hate it when Ruthie wears that white shirt with that purple sweater.*

On the way home from Calvert's my mother pulled out and turned right into traffic, but either an approaching driver had sped up or she had forgotten to look left before turning. The other driver, a man, opened his window and said, *You should learn to look where you're going,* and my mother said, *Okay,* and I felt sweaty. I wanted the man's car to catch fire so I could watch him burn. It was a long time before I understood why my mother knew instinctively to wilt under his accusatory heat.

One Saturday we were in the usual tavern for lunch; my parents loved bar food. My mother and I sat side by side on a vinyl-covered bench, and my mother spread her skirt out on both sides so it wouldn't crease. When she fluffed her skirt it lightly brushed my bare leg. One of her swollen feet, squeezed into its little shoe, rested next to mine like a cat curling up next to another cat. Yet these touches felt violent.

I had to slide away and stand up to crush the discomfort in my brain, and as I stood there shuddering, my mother looked at me with hateful joy. *Now everyone's looking at you,* she said. I looked around the room, and everyone was.

When my parents came home from their high school reunion, I asked them if everyone else had gone. I knew all their stories. I wanted to hear about the greaser who went with the cheap girls with teased hair. I wanted to hear about the boy who had asked my mother to the senior prom.

*—He came up to where I was sitting and said hello, but I just looked down at the table and didn't say anything.—Why not?—Well, I couldn't talk to him, there, in front of everyone!*

She thought that everyone had come to the reunion to watch her attend the reunion.

———

The market, the movies, the school play—it didn't matter. My mother's first question was always the same. *Was it crowded?*

She didn't care who saw her fear. Or she didn't think she was revealing anything. Or she didn't think she was afraid.

My mother had gone to college out west, near the New York border, and returned home two weeks later because she'd forgotten all her blouses and because it was too far out in the country, she explained. I didn't understand what she meant by this, but she stated it with such finality that I couldn't conceive of asking a question. She was calm. Her voice sounded kind, as if what she was saying didn't even need explaining, since it was already so clear.

I imagine that she was held taut at the end of a thread connecting her to her mother and father and sister and home, and that she couldn't possibly stay so far away for long. I never thought about all the other girls who must have been at college, too, just as far away from home or farther. My mother never mentioned them. That she had left home to go to a place so far away that it was almost in another state—that was part of her legend.

3

The local library, white clapboard with green shutters, had once been a one-room schoolhouse. Boys and girls had lined up at its two green doors thirty years before the town was even a town.

I scratched gray stones against the bricks in the path. They smelled like gunpowder. Bright green moss swelled between the bricks.

Next to the library was a little garden bounded by a forsythia hedge that exploded annually into a wall of yellow stars. The gap in the hedge wasn't hard to find, and I went back and forth between the lawn and the garden while my mother sat on a bench and read a romance novel with silver lettering on the cover. I dug up the earthworms and chased the beetles and once, when I put my hand down, it went into a soft wet mound and came up with the bright stink of shit. Someone had let a dog into the garden. My mother led me into the library's little bathroom and wiped off the shit with little squares of toilet paper and washed my hand and dried it with paper towels. Then she held my hand to her nose and sniffed and made a face.

On Saturdays my father and I went to the dump.

I walked up the hill to the shed where people left old books, and I took as many as I wanted back to the car, which my father had already filled with half-broken furniture.

After that, we rode all over town to hit the garage sales advertised in the *Courier*. I always had enough time to pick up and examine everything. Sometimes I bought a little ceramic animal or an LP with the two dollars' allowance I was given every Sunday. We never went to the better part of town, because rich people didn't have garage sales—they just brought their things to the dump.

Once, after finding a listing in the *Courier,* my mother drove me to buy a camp trunk.

There were greener trees and bigger houses in that neighborhood, and fewer American flags. I don't remember anything about the inside of the house, but I remember a woman opening the trunk with a sense of ceremony that clashed with the torn paper lining where her daughter had peeled away her stickers. The cardboard tray on top was warped. The woman's face was smooth and serene. She wore a headband, and her hair curled immaculately under her chin. My mother gave her thirty dollars. By the time we were back in the car, my mother was sputtering that that was the retail price of the trunk, and that I could have had a new one for just as much.

On weeknights we went to Extras, where there was free coffee for my father and a giant warehouse full of damaged inventory and overstock—books, clothes, shoes, rugs, chairs, and anything else you could think of. The front room sold fruit. Each time we went we found a new surprise, a rack of sequined gowns or a six-foot-wide tub full of balloons. One year I chose a different balloon for every girl who came to my birthday party. My mother blew them all up and held their strings in her hand, and everyone had to pull a string, and the girl who pulled the heart-shaped balloon won a prize.

Sometimes my mother and I went to the health food store if we had another errand to do in that neighborhood. We called the just-past-ripe shelf of discounted produce the Used Food section. *Go and get a soda and meet me over in the used food!* my mother called to me, forgetting we weren't alone. *It isn't used!* scolded a ropy stocker.

My mother was never embarrassed to buy those soft peaches going brown, and when I had to bring an extra pair of shoes to school for gym class, she took me to buy a pair of Keds in an unsellable beige, marked down to two dollars; neither of us understood the need for "athletic" shoes. I painted little stars and moons all over them and replaced the laces with black ribbons, and when classmates gently complimented me on my handiwork, I offered to "do" their sneakers up the same way. They all had proper running shoes and wore the same expensive windbreaker in different colors.

In the classroom we placed sheets of black paper over a per- forated metal screen, turned on the light, and pushed little translucent plastic pins through the paper. Such beauty— stars, rainbows, bunches of glowing grapes.

I asked my parents to buy me a Lite Brite like the one I played with in school, and they did. It was the only toy I had that plugged in, that was bought new, and that came in its original box with all its parts. No one had ever played with it before!

I couldn't reconcile it with the other things in my room and in our house, and I can't remember ever playing with it. It was mine, but I didn't feel worthy of using it. It wasn't my turn to use it yet, not when it was still brand-new. This was true not just of toys and bikes but of the land beneath us. It had belonged to the settlers, who gave it to our town as a gift when they didn't want it anymore. Now it was ours.

The fact that we hadn't had to pay for it was what made it so valuable.

———

We drank powdered milk and never threw away food.

My mother did most of the shopping at the gas station around the corner, past the fundamentalist church. The little market had potato salad and cabbage slaw in tubs. It had lettuce and bananas. It had cans and spice packets and breakfast cereal in boxes and bags. The aisles were narrow and the shelves were short enough that I could almost see over them.

I ate a bag of crackers for lunch and a box of macaroni and cheese for supper. Sometimes I got a taco flavoring packet and some taco shells and some ground meat and went to town with diced American cheese and chopped iceberg lettuce.

My mother drank Diet Pepsi and Tab and peeled the thin Styrofoam labels off the glass bottles with her pink-brown painted nails. She made chicken divan with a can of chicken and a can of mushroom soup. She cooked unseasoned hamburger patties in a pan until they were dark brown. She steamed whole potatoes in the microwave. On Wednesdays, when I came home from school before lunch, she heated up some alphabet soup and toasted an English muffin with two dollops of ketchup and two slices of American cheese melted over the top in the toaster oven.

The refrigerator always had a brown plastic pitcher of iced tea made from powder and a pink plastic pitcher of pink lemonade made from powder and a clear plastic pitcher of orange juice made from frozen concentrate. We only drank that in the morning.

My mother baked brownies, cakes, and cookies. She used a heavy-bottomed orange cooking pot to make butterscotch and chocolate sauces. *I'm so fat,* she said. *Tomorrow starts my diet,* she said, sucking chocolate off her fingers. *Tomorrow starts my diet,* she said, waiting for applause.

I liked to buy candy at the drugstore and walk across the street to the cemetery of the Congregational church, where three-hundred-year-old babies lay in the earth beside their aged parents. I chewed a spice drop and thought about the dead people.

My own girlhood felt like something from 1650 even when it was happening. The little parties, kindnesses done by friends, the light as I walked home from school. Pine needles. I spent those days feeling half-there, not quite committed to that life.

It was peaceful there, among the stones. And it was peaceful on my street, where the old people wore the same faces the dead ones had had, the ones who had built the houses two hundred years before. Look, there they are in the portraits hanging next to the stairs. You can see them at night, from the road, through translucent curtains.

———

My mother hung antique prints of George Washington and Abraham Lincoln on the walls as if we lived inside a schoolgirl's report on the United States of America. The fact that some of them were ugly or damaged was beside the point. My parents weren't after shiny things or even beautiful things; they simply liked getting the things that stupid people threw away.

We didn't display any photographs of ourselves, even on the refrigerator. My friends' houses had photographs of themselves on the walls and on the refrigerators, and I wondered why we didn't, but I also understood that George Washington was more important than anyone in my family.

My mother found a fancy wristwatch catalog in the book swap at the dump. The front cover was crumpled, but she ironed it, as she ironed crumpled dollar bills. On the coffee table, next to a glass bowl from a garage sale, it looked like something a rich person would have. She set it just askew on the table, as if someone had been reading it and carelessly put it down, and she corrected its angle when she walked by.

Our bookcases held shiny hardcover books, bestsellers from a decade ago or more. The main quality my parents sought in books was that they were free at the book swap, and that their jackets were intact, as if they'd been bought at a store. No one read them, not even me. Then there were a few mass-market paperbacks of classics that my parents had kept from high school, and some other bestsellers of the 1950s with cracked spines that someone must have read at one point.

My mother's romance novels from the library didn't interest me. I liked stories about orphans or runaways, especially the ones that explained exactly how to build a shelter inside a giant tree or in a cave or in the side of a mountain. I often left the last few pages unread for days, straining to extend the experience. My parents always noticed my laminated bookmarks, with their little yarn tassels, sticking out of my library books, with only a fraction of an inch of pages left to read. They laughed at me.

Their little book on collectibles said that fake lithographs were easily identified under a magnifying glass. If you could see spots, it said, the picture was a reprint, not a true lithograph. At a consignment shop in a nearby town, my father took off his glasses and leaned close to a picture and squinted and bared his teeth. No dots! He was going to pay fifty dollars for a large-format print.

The picture was a reprint. I could see the dots. And I could see that my father wanted so much to believe the picture was a real antique, it didn't matter that the dots were there. He would never see them.

I caught the bug, too. When everyone in school bought thirty-dollar Swatch watches, I sent away for a free watch from Tropicana after collecting enough proofs of purchase from the frozen cans of concentrate my mother bought. The little orange watch had white hands and a white plastic strap, and each section of the orange measured five minutes on its face. I knew the watch was garbage, but it had been free, and besides, no one else in school had one.

———

My mother smeared orange cream on her face and left a line like a mask. She took the little brush from her compact, ran a dribble of water over it, and painted a gray line on each of her eyelids, right above where the eyelashes grew. Then she held a mascara wand near each eye and blinked. Then she opened a tube of red-brown lipstick and colored her top lip and then the bottom one.

I too had a little makeup kit: a fuchsia lipstick in a sample size, some tawny foundation, and a purple eyeshadow compact with a little mirror and a foam-tipped swab. I had pink nail polish and maroon nail polish and clear nail polish with silver flecks. I kept all of these things, and an empty purple perfume bottle my grandmother had given me, on a plastic tray made to look like mother-of-pearl.

My mother kept a shoebox full of jewelry on the floor of her closet and another shoebox full of old makeup. When I was three and had to dance in a ballet recital, my mother took some things out of the shoebox and painted bright pink lipstick and rouge and blue eyeshadow onto my face. The old lipstick tasted sour.

I don't remember the dancing, but I remember the stage being quite dark, even though it was the middle of the day, and I remember being backstage with a girl in a yellow tutu. She grabbed her yellow straps and threw them down so that she was suddenly naked. She looked at me. On her face I saw pure fear.

I don't remember any of the steps we learned, but I remember that in every ballet class, we had to start out standing on a little white painted X on the floor and then skip around the room, and when the piano player stopped, we had to run back to the same X we'd started from. Everyone else could tell their little white X from all the others. I don't know how they did it.

———

Our next-door neighbors had a new baby. My mother and I went to take care of the tiny boy while his mother went to the doctor. I had never been so close to a baby before.

We sat in the little nursery, where the baby lay on his back in his crib on a soft white cloth. When he burped, a bit of white fluid fell from his mouth, down his cheek, to the white cloth underneath. My mother removed the cloth and wiped his mouth with it and put the cloth in a nearby bin and put down a fresh cloth.

Then we sat back and watched the baby to see what he would do, and in another moment he burped again and drooled some more white drool onto the cloth. And my mother removed that cloth, with its tiny wet patch, and put it in the bin and placed another cloth under the leaky little creature.

After three or four more changes I looked at the pile of barely spotted, barely marked cloths in the bin. We sat and stared and waited for the baby to burp again. He stared back. His big eyes, watching. His silence. His little silent burps and his tolerance while my mother pulled him up by his legs and tugged the quilted cloth out from under him and put a new one down.

My mother was vigilant, tense in her chair, ready to move if the baby burped again. I could see that she was proud of the speed at which she witnessed the seepage and replaced the cloth, barely touching the boy. As if to let him lie on a spotted cloth was the lowest form of neglect. As if to touch him would lessen her efficiency.

Watching us watching him. Big eyes. All three of us, silent. Three pairs of eyes, watching. The mountain of quilted cloths. A faint odor of sour milk.

What was the story of my being born? I asked my mother.

I knew only that I'd been cut out of her. That my mother had had one contraction and that labor had stopped, and then there was nothing left to do but cut.

The doctor said, *Oh, she's beautiful,* when he pulled me out, and my mother had thought he was talking about her.

Sometimes when my mother told the story she drew the side of her hand horizontally across her belly like a knife. I never saw the scar.

What was I like when I was a baby? My mother told me that a lady had stayed in my parents' house until I was four weeks old, taking care of me, day and night.

In nursery school the teachers had thought I was deaf because I never responded to their prompts to speak. My parents always laughed when they remembered asking me, after meeting with the nursery school teachers, *Can you talk?* And I answered, *Yes.* What a funny child.

My mother said that when I was two years old, she and my father went to Maine for a week and hired a woman to stay with me, and that when they returned I said to them, *You came back!* In my nightmares my parents abandoned me, over and over. In the dream, I cried out, *Dear Mother! Dear Father!*

In all of my earliest memories I am alone in my crib. I have no memories of being held. But I do remember closing my eyes in absolute pleasure while my mother stroked my head. Did she do it more than once? I asked her to do it again, all the time, and she always said no. What unwanted touch did it recall for her?

4

*Do you know any swears?* my mother asked. It was evening and I was brushing my teeth in the little blue-and-black-tiled bathroom. It was dark in the hall, dark outside the window. My mother was smiling like a big sister. I knew all the swears just from listening to my parents yell at each other. *Do you know how to spell* fuck? she asked, her eyes narrowing with delight. *F-U-C-H*, I said, remembering what I'd seen somewhere on a wall. But no, it was *F-U-C-K*, my mother said. *Do you know what it means?* she asked with a sly look. I didn't say anything.

In kindergarten we'd had to draw pictures of two things we were thankful for, and I'd chosen *My Mother* and *Balloons*.

My mother liked to play cards, and she loved to win. When she wasn't ahead by a mile, if she was just winning by a few points, she complained that she'd been dealt a terrible hand, that she was always dealt the worst hand. When it was anyone else's turn, she seethed, *Hurry up!*

When I suggested that we play Scrabble instead of cards, she said, *I'll probably just lose again.* Then, just before she did lose again, she knocked my father's tiles onto the table and yelled, *You're dropping peanut crumbs onto the floor!* There were no peanut crumbs on the floor.

She went into the kitchen and stuffed a slice of cake into her mouth and stood at the window until she finished swallowing it.

The day before she started a new diet, my mother took a big bowl of potato salad out of the refrigerator and shoveled big bites into her mouth. She ate other things, too. She ate everything in the refrigerator, fast, as if someone were about to take it away from her, or as if she were afraid to think about it for fear she might stop. She complained all her life about constipation.

After a year of dieting, my mother stopped buying the special frozen meals, and she stopped eating lettuce wedges with a sprinkle of seasoned salt from a packet. She gained back all the weight.

*I was TOO thin,* she often said of that thrilling year of postponing her appetites, as if she were exposing some terrible truth for the first time. She had just been slightly less fat.

She wore velour pants and jackets and called it a *suit.* You could see the lines of her underwear under it. She liked to wear the smallest size she could squeeze into.

She said, *All the old men smile at me. It used to be the young men.*

———

When I was old enough to read and write, I started writing a musical. I thought of a sad princess, the depthless sky mirroring her loneliness. When a fairy asked the princess what she wanted, the princess sang a song about wanting a husband. I called the play *The Sebastian Princess* and hid the notebook under my bed.

*She just wants a husband,* my mother said to me after finding my little notebook, as if disappointed there hadn't been more to the story, as if I had written it for her, to her, and placed the notebook in her hands.

———

I often took naps on my father's side of the bed, falling asleep inhaling his scent from the yellowing foam pillow. In the evenings I crawled between my parents to lean against the heavy wooden headboard that I called a *bedboard*. My father often said, *The bed is not a playpen!* angrily, if I brought a book to read in the big bed, next to my mother. She never said anything.

Often I would wake in the night to the sound of the headboard banging against the wall, and call out to my parents to stop. I imagined them flopping their big bodies around in the hot air, on a summer night, watching television, trying to get comfortable. I was annoyed that they were so clumsy about it.

That summer we stayed in a sunny room in a rented condominium on the Cape. My parents slept in one double bed and I slept in the other one, two feet away.

My mother's legs splayed out in a V under the covers. She wore cheap shiny nightgowns that poorly concealed her lumpy body. She loved to lift the nightgown high up over her thighs, showing off the blue and red veins. I begged her to cover herself. She said, *You're such a prude!*

I woke up one morning to my parents whispering. It was hot, and we had all kicked the covers off. My father was on his back and my mother was sitting next to him, her back against the headboard.

My father was lying quite still, but in the middle of his pale blue pajamas was a wriggling, as if a little animal needed to get out. Inside his pants his penis rose and fell, shuddering as it moved. Then my mother swung her legs over the side of the bed and leaned back so that she lay over the middle of my father and her back concealed his naughty penis.

———

On hot days my mother took us to her parents' apartment complex, where there was a pool. My grandfather was always there, waiting in a short chair, reading. Every now and then he'd lift himself up from the chair slowly, like an elephant, though he was bony and stooped, not elephantine. He walked slowly down the steps of the pool on his hammertoes and submerged. Then he went back to his chair and picked his book back up. He must have watched me swim, but I never paid attention.

Sometimes my mother and I went up to her parents' apartment afterward. They kept a glass jar filled with jelly beans, and I was allowed to have as many as I wanted.

My grandmother was usually there, in the apartment, walking slowly and dreamily from room to room, her slippers scuffing along the creaky parquet floor. She carried handfuls of jelly beans and put them carelessly into her mouth, all at once. Imagining the apricot and mint and coffee flavors all mixed up made me cringe.

If my grandmother came down to the pool, she walked the same slow, uncertain walk, and sat on a long chair and rubbed bright orange lotion, squeezed from a metal tube, into her arms and legs. It smelled like cake batter.

Once, at home, I ran around the backyard while my mother sprayed me with the garden hose. I laughed so hard I thought I might burst. Many times after that I asked my mother to spray me with the hose again, but she always said no. She didn't say it angrily or impatiently; she said it dreamily, as if she were under a spell that prevented her from causing such dangerous delight. I thought that maybe it was wrong to be that loudly happy, and that she was trying to protect me.

———

One night we all went to the movies. My mother bought a box of candy and a cup of popcorn and nothing to drink. She opened the candy and threw the plastic wrapper on the floor of the theater. I picked it up. She looked at me as if I'd just done something stupid.

She put the popcorn cup on the floor between her feet and leaned back in her chair and held on to the insides of her ripply thighs, her fingers reaching down and around them. Every few moments, one of her hands twitched. She closed her eyes halfway and rubbed her tongue all around her teeth. One of her knees rested softly next to mine.

When the movie was over, she kicked her popcorn cup under the chair in front of her.

On the way home I learned that we had left the house only because my mother had decided not to attend our neighbors' Christmas party. She'd thought that they would notice our car was gone.

I don't remember anything about the movie.

At recess that day I had jumped rope with the other girls. I was thinking about the rope held at both ends by two girls who gaily threw it over my head when it was my turn to jump, the rhymes we chanted, the coats we wore, our rubber boots marked with salt from the icy sidewalks. Sometimes I took a crunchy walk home from school over gray ice, and at an intersection, at a blocked gutter, I stepped onto the ice and it would be a slush puddle a foot deep and evilly cold.

One afternoon the brook path was iced over. I fell flat on my back and couldn't stand up again and crawled up to the street and walked down the middle of the street to the market and put a dime in a pay phone and called my mother. Or maybe I didn't have a dime and called collect. She screamed at me and said that she had never gotten a ride home from school. But she had grown up in the city, where the sidewalks were shoveled. I crawled and tiptoed home.

It was almost my birthday. My mother bought me a sateen slip dotted with little pink and red hearts, and at my birthday party I wore it under my skirt. I also got a new flannel nightgown. Under the covers it released sparks, a cold little fireworks show.

That year my birthday party was a few days after a historic blizzard. Driving was still banned, so my father walked to the store and bought a cake and dragged it home on my sled. My friends walked over with their grateful, snowed-in parents. My mother helped us make construction-paper crowns, which we all wore.

In a photograph from that day, I'm standing next to a pile left by the town plows, and it's more than twice my height.

———

*It's zero degrees,* a girl said during recess, as if it were a scientific impossibility, an idea that none of us had ever had. *It's zero degrees.* It was often zero degrees. No one cared. Our woolen mittens got soppy while we played. *It's zero degrees.* When someone finally responded, she did so softly, like a black bear not quite waking all the way up. *No, it's one below.*

Wearing a warm coat over my Brownie uniform, I stood at evergreen-draped doors and asked people to sign my card and pledge two dollars for a box of Thin Mints or Trefoils. I'd deliver the cookies later in the season, when there was still enough snow on the ground that I'd need to wear plastic produce bags in my boots, over my socks. Even then, sometimes I got a chilblain that stayed hot and red for the rest of the day.

After a few houses the ballpoint pen started to skip and trail dark blue blobs. After the ink in the reservoir froze solid, someone gave me a pencil, and I kept going.

The school flooded the playing fields after Halloween and the water froze into an ice rink. One year I fell on the field and knocked out a tooth.

A two-story mass of plowed snow stood in the far end of the schoolyard. We dug slides and caverns and stairs, little hollows to store things, sticks and icicles and snowballs that melted and refroze. Our hands were pink and wet and red. On our side of the snow mass we had a password to enter, S *and* P, snow and plaster, and a hand gesture that went with it.

When the duck pond froze, the geese came and got in line like children and took turns sliding on a spot they'd melted slick with their warm blubbery bottoms.

One day, after a fresh snow, I lay supine on the snow-bedded picnic table and stared up into the black branches high above me, the sky blue and white beyond that. It was so quiet; the snow muffled the little sounds of the neighborhood. *What are you doing!* my mother screamed out the kitchen window. I extracted myself from the me-shaped hole, my cold, clean, aboveground grave.

The salted snow left white lines on the flagstones, and even if you poured hot water over them and scrubbed, as my mother did each spring, those ghosts of winter never quite disappeared.

# 5

Bannon Road had ten two-story brick buildings, each with ten apartments inside. The playground at the end of the road was just big enough to hold a swing set and a dented metal slide. When the sun was out the slide got too bright to look at.

Most of the kids who lived in the Bannon Road projects lived with one parent and a lot of siblings, or with grandparents, or with a mother and an aunt and a baby cousin. All of the Bannon Road kids were in the Special Ed class, but together on the playground at school you couldn't have guessed who lived where until you heard them speak. The Bannon Road kids had Boston accents, which is to say the accents of the poor. My mother spoke with an accent, too, but it was imitation Brahmin, all *muhthahs* and *bahthtubs*.

My friend Amber lived where I did, across town from Bannon Road. Our trees were blue-gray Douglas firs and crab-apples that no one picked, so the fruit got tracked half a block down from where it fell.

Amber and her extended family had moved up to Massachusetts from North Carolina. All of her clothes and shoes were already worn, and she got strips of free school lunch tickets like the Bannon Road kids. She lived on the only dirt road in town, and the front yard had just enough room for two cars on cement blocks.

Amber's father was a mechanic, but not in the way that other people's fathers were lawyers or bankers. The other fathers were what they were only at work, in offices in the city, and while visible in our town they were just fathers. Her father was a mechanic even at home, with his tools and his overalls.

The first time Amber came over I noticed the cloud of charisma that clung around her despite her poor teeth and thin clothes.

*He's a hunka cheese!* Amber said, sitting with me at the kitchen table after school, eating a snack, talking about boys. I threw a grape at her. It hit her right in her open eye. She ran to the bathroom to rinse it out.

My mother was at the table with us. She glared at me, not for inadvertently hurting my friend but for not being boy-crazy like Amber. She wanted to talk about boys, too.

When it was time for Amber to go home, I followed her out the front door and down the steps. When she got back onto her too-big orange Huffy, she saw that I was crying. I was desperate to stop, but I couldn't. I had no thoughts; it was my body that was crying. I cried as she rode away. The shame, the surprise, came like a slap. Until then I hadn't known I was lonely.

When I showed my mother Amber's birthday party invitation, which was typed on a slip of pink paper, my mother said, approvingly, *You couldn't do this.* She liked Amber's refusal to be ashamed of her poverty, her ability to do things that only poor kids were resourceful enough to do. My mother seemed to admire Amber, but she also aspired to be better. Maybe my mother liked having her around because compared with Amber, we weren't poor.

One afternoon Amber brought over a plastic bag full of her sisters' old makeup—creamy rouge and blue and green eye shadows and mascara. Everything came in little tubes, even some wet pink lipstick swabs.

I'd seen my mother blink in front of a mascara wand, so I held one in front of my eye and blinked and felt my eyelashes hit the wand. I knew how to put on mascara! I blinked again and again, practicing, the little hairs getting cakey. I dusted a big soft brush on a pink circle of pressed powder and drew big pink circles on my cheeks. The brush felt wonderful, like the end of a cat's tail. I swished it around.

When my mother came upstairs and said that it was time for Amber to go home, we filled her bag with all the makeup, and Amber picked it up as if it were nothing. She walked out the door and said goodbye, and in the next moment my mother said that we had to go and do errands. I wanted to wash my face, but there was no time. No time—did she even notice my face? But my mother didn't say a thing. Maybe I looked the same to her. Maybe I was the only one who could see the pink and purple blotches I'd painted on.

We parked on the street in front of the little market, just behind the blue mailbox. I wasn't allowed to stay in the car; my mother made me go with her while she shopped. Standing at the cashier's counter, I didn't even watch the girl key in the prices with her fast fingers. I turned away, my back to the cashier, trying to point my face in a direction from which no one could see it. I felt exposed. I wondered if I was being punished.

———

Most of the time Amber came to my house, where it was just me and my mother; I went to her house seldom, but it was always an event. I once went there with some neighborhood kids for sauce. When we arrived we were each given a bowl of tomato sauce and a spoon. The room was dark and noisy, the house simmering with life.

Amber had a niece who was our age, and we three played together. Amber's sisters were older. They sat on the concrete steps and mixed torn-up grass with water in plastic containers, using fat sticks to stir the greening liquid. They were trying to get the water as green as they could. It seemed childish to me, but then I looked at their faces and saw that they thought they were working, not playing. They didn't think they were children anymore.

On our way home from school, Amber and I goosed each other. *Go ahead!* I giggled. *High society walks first!* I said it without thinking. I wanted her to walk in front so I could keep pinching her.

*I'm not high society,* she said, looking right into my eyes. She was so calm. *I'm low society, and I'm damn proud of it.*

Her certainty filled her.

For a needle-thin, silver flash of a moment, I felt embarrassed for my friend. Then I felt embarrassed for myself, living in that town, playing at belonging.

About halfway down the road from school was the marsh, which occupied three lots between some houses and the

Baptist church. And in the wildflowers and cattails were five men in work clothes and rubber boots, digging a hole. Amber asked the men what they were digging. *A swimming pool,* one of them said, smiling wide.

I'd never been told not to talk with men digging holes in swamps, so I told my mother about the men and the hole. When I told the story I told it with pity for the men, who really did seem to think they were being funny, or that they'd been hired to dig a swimming pool; either way they were pitiable, and not just because they had to squelch around in the smelly swamp.

My mother scolded me for speaking to them. She seemed less furious than frightened.

———

When it rained on a school day, my mother stayed in bed, as usual, and other people's mothers picked me up along the way as I walked. I sat damp and apologetic in the backseat, my backpack pitching me forward.

Sixteen kids sat in a circle on a mat. After Show and Tell the teacher said, *Fifteen students participated in Show and Tell today.* Then, a soft flurry, and someone quickly said, *Ruthie! She never shares.* Then our big pink teacher spoke slowly and with great pleasure, *Ruth will share when she is ready to share.*

The teacher smiled meanly, as if expecting to prod me into speaking, but I wasn't keeping anything from her, or from anyone—I was simply a person who had nothing to share, nothing worth sharing. I pitied the teacher for assuming I was like the other children.

That year we didn't have a lavatory in the classroom anymore. We had to go out into the hall, which was always too dark, and turn left and walk up to the girls' bathroom and push open the door into the tiled room that was even darker until you turned the light on. I was more afraid of the dark than I was of being seen on the toilet, so I always used the first stall, closest to the outer door. For some reason that stall had no door of its own, so anyone who came into the bathroom could see me. If the outer door swung open while I was on the toilet, I always grabbed at my clothes and tried to cover my lap, but when I saw that it was only another girl, I meekly let go of my pants and kept on pissing. I never remembered who had seen me; I imagined the outer door was a memory-erasing apparatus.

A few months into the year, a girl came in and saw me and said, with irritation, *You always use that one!* I was surprised that she knew me. I'd thought I was invisible.

———

Officer Hill visited the school every fall and told us to register our bikes at the precinct. If you paid twenty-five cents for a shiny blue sticker, your bike would never get stolen. A thief would see the sticker and just give up.

There was a messiness about Officer Hill, a lure, a spillage, like eyeliner weeping down the face, like an animal giving off a scent. Like prey. As if he'd wanted whatever had happened to him all along. He had a hoarse, high voice, and he wore his gun on a belt around his waist. The gun and the belt were black, and his pants were blue. The belt hung oddly low.

He paced in front of us while we sat on the polished floor of the gym. He said he hated how easy it would be for someone to hurt one of us, to pick one of us off like a sick little animal. *It would be so easy,* he said. He spoke much too loudly. He was there, he said, to protect us. He seemed to be strutting *at* us, taunting us. He arched his back so that when he walked, he moved forward hips-first, gun-first.

The second year that Officer Hill came to the school gym he asked us if we remembered how much it cost to register a bicycle at the precinct, and I raised my hand. *A candy bar is thirty-five cents and registering your bike is twenty-five cents,* I recited, expecting to be praised.

He looked at me and didn't say anything. His eyes closed a little. I could tell he didn't like me. This is what I figured out: If we remembered the script, he wouldn't have to come back to school again.

When he was at school on regular days, as the Youth Officer, Officer Hill spent most of his time with the Bannon Road kids. They were the poorest in town and were assumed to have the most problems, or to have the sorts of problem that only a cop could fix. Beyond registering bikes and giving out parking tickets, I didn't know what sort of problems a cop could fix. And I knew plenty of kids who had problems and didn't live on Bannon Road.

After Officer Hill told me I'd given the right answer, he spent a long time telling us never to get into a car with a stranger. That we should only ever get into a car driven by our parents, or an adult we knew well, or an officer of the law. Where were these officers of the law, driving around, waiting to help us?

Amber told me that she had walked most of the way home from school one day and gotten tired and asked a mailman to drive her the rest of the way in his funny right-hand-drive truck with no doors. In the end we couldn't decide whether the mailman counted as a stranger or not, but Amber said that the stripes on his truck were red, white, and blue, so he had to be a good guy. Amber's parents didn't notice when she came home late or when her older brother tickled her until she dropped her towel.

———

Shortly after that visit we heard that Officer Hill had spanked a boy on his naked bottom and kissed him on the mouth, but the kiss must have been an accident. Every day of first grade, I imagined getting into fights with the boys in my class, falling onto the floor, wrestling under the table, and then kissing them by accident.

We then heard that the accuser had been a Bannon Road kid, but everyone said that the charges were impossible. If Officer Hill had been kissing and spanking kids, someone would have stopped him.

About a week later Officer Hill got shot. We all heard the same story a few times, from different kids, and pretty soon everyone knew. Officer Hill had been shot, and he had died. The bell rang. We started walking purposefully to our homerooms.

Then we heard that Officer Hill had called the other police officers on his radio and, with his other hand, shot himself in the head. He did it on his front lawn.

My mother said that it was so sad that the officer had had to kill himself.

Still, his swagger—I knew that he hated us. *Had* hated us.

———

After Officer Hill was dead and buried, there was a second investigation, and the result was published in the *Courier*.

The Bannon Road kid had lied. He hadn't been kissed on the lips or spanked on his bare bottom at all; Officer Hill had spanked him through his pants, and then kissed him on the forehead to console him about the spanking.

A priest was quoted in the newspaper article. *If Hill's guilty of anything it's of being too generous. At another time he would have been lauded for trying to be a father to this wretched child.*

Once, a Bannon Road girl had kicked me in the cheekbone at recess one day and then afterward told our kindergarten teacher, *Ruthie kicked me right here,* pointing to the spot on her own cheek.

So a Bannon Road kid was liable to make up a story like the one the boy had told. He was liable to be a bad, sneaky kid, and full of lies.

## 6

Bee was the last girl in the class to learn how to jump rope, write in cursive, and put her chair up on her desk. She had long yellow hair and pink freckles.

Bee's mother had a big gap between her teeth and a face like a basset hound's. She had sent Bee to kindergarten a year early, in impeccable braids.

Bee stared just to the side of wherever we were meant to direct our attention, her mouth slightly open. While the teacher showed us how to draw a five-pointed star, Bee surreptitiously licked the blue paper of her crayon all the way around, soaking it. It was one of the kindergarten crayons, flat on one side.

Bee and I walked down a wooded alley to school, lined on both sides by angry, chained dogs. We once saw a smaller dog running free, a beard of foam hanging from his chin.

One morning Bee found the cardboard tab from a Red Rose tea bag, the kind I drank at home, at night, loaded with sugar, when my stomach hurt. *Look, a rose!* she said, as if it were real. I said, *That's trash. Give it to me.* I was suddenly angry.

She looked at me, dubious, so I changed my tone.—*It's so pretty. Can I see it?*

Then she gave it to me. I tore it in half and then in half again while Bee wailed.—*It's dirty! It's dirty trash!* My anger surprised me. I hated her, and I didn't know why.

———

One day after lunch, when some of us got back to class early, some mean girls hid Bee's schoolbag in an old file drawer in the back of the classroom. Why pick on Bee? I couldn't think about anything else for the rest of the day.

At the end of the day Bee announced that she couldn't find her bag. I could feel my heart beating. I looked down at my desk. Our teacher sighed and looked bored. *Does anyone know about this?* she asked. The threat of a giggle bubbled up like a burp. I covered for it by opening my eyes wide and shrugging my shoulders. Surely that's what I would do if I didn't know where Bee's bag was. I shrugged and raised my eyebrows. Was I doing it convincingly enough? I raised my eyebrows higher. I needed the teacher to see me from the front of the room. I needed her to see how little I knew about what possibly could have happened to Bee's bag.

The teacher called my name. It was so loud, I would re-member it forever. I looked at her and she looked at me. She could see that I wasn't brave enough to come clean. *Bee and I will leave the room,* she said, *and when we come back that bag had better be on that hook.* They left the room.

A girl got up and ran frantically down the room to retrieve the bag from its hiding place. She opened one of the two big doors of the coat closet and hung up the bag and ran back to her seat. She and her mean, clever friends breathed some words to each other that I couldn't hear. For a few mo-ments we all waited. I was breathing hard. Then the teacher opened the door. The bag was there, on its hook, as if it had been there all along. The teacher slowly blinked her eyes, shut the closet door, and didn't say anything else about it.

———

Bee had a tiled swimming pool in her backyard, and she told me she was allowed to sleep in the pool, drifting on a floating chair. I knew that she was lying, but I didn't know why she would lie about something so obvious. And I didn't think she was lying when she told me that she and her father still took showers together. Still? I'd never seen my father naked. Or my mother.

When I went to Bee's house, we went into her room and closed the door. She and I practiced tackling each other. *Honey, I'm home!* she'd say, and then she'd shut an invisible door as if it were the door of our house and tackle me. I didn't feel much, not even when we sat together and read aloud, side by side on the floor, scratching at the seams of each other's jeans.

At one point Bee's father let himself into Bee's room and Bee ran out and I stayed there. Her father looked at me and smiled and said, *Having fun?*

In third grade Bee gave me a red umbrella with tiny white dots. I loved sliding it open like a big flower, and I danced with it in the backyard even when it wasn't raining. I loved that umbrella and I loved the flowered lunch box that another friend had given me. Such useful things.

Many of the other things the girls brought to my birthday parties, stationery sets and pencils and stickers, my mother and I carefully set aside to give to other girls when they had their birthday parties.

Amber wasn't in Brownies with me, but Bee was. On Tuesdays we wore our uniforms to school, our sashes studded with badges and pins.

In my catalog of Girl Scout things, the Senior Scouts looked like mothers and wore green polyester outfits with jackets and little scarves. In some of the pictures the Brownies wore jersey shortie nightgowns and held their hands, loosely clasped, in front of their pubic mounds. I strained to see the outlines of their panties, but the girls were naked under those nighties. Under my breath I mispronounced the word *insignia* as the beautiful word *in-SIGN-ah*.

———

Almost every girl had a three-ring binder with sticky cardboard pages. The books were photo albums, but we carefully arranged our best stickers, mounted on squares of wax paper, on the sticky pages, and then smoothed the plastic film back over them. I invited girls over after school chiefly to obtain new stickers.

Even the dullest girls had sticker collections, and the dullness of the girl didn't correlate with the dullness of her stickers, so when I heard that Bee had a sticker collection, I said, *I didn't know you had a sticker book. Do you want to come over?* She did. And the next day at school, she gave me a thank-you note.

The following year the girls all gave each other silver wire rings. Another year we gave each other barrettes with our names on them in tiny white stickers.

No one gave Bee a pair of name barrettes; the store didn't have any that said BEE or BEATRICE. My mother bought some barrettes and some enamel paints and some of the tiny stickers, and she made Bee a pair of purple barrettes with little white hearts surrounding the letters.

My mother practiced painting the hearts on a piece of yellow scrap paper. She dipped her brush into the blue enamel and made a row of perfect hearts. They looked like something that had come out of a machine. I ached with admiration.

I couldn't bear to let the practice hearts go into the trash, so I took the slip of paper and saved it in my shoebox of special things.

The following year we all gave each other friendship pins, tiny beads on safety pins, and wore them on our sneakers.

We all collected beads and stickers shaped like hearts and pencils that smelled like strawberries. Everything smelled like strawberries then—stickers, lip gloss, hair.

Bee and I sat together and made friendship pins one after-noon, dozens of different designs. She had a box lined with black velvet, and when her parents held a garage sale, she sold her pins for a quarter each.

That was the year that all the girls bought little pouches of plastic or foil confetti for each other. Tiny metallic discs in every color; tiny plastic hearts in iridescent pink; even tinier stars and sticks, squares and diamonds, in gold and silver and red and black. I collected a lot of it; we enclosed it in birthday cards and the confetti fell out and made a little surprise party. The bits were big enough to pick up and put back in the envelope.

When the fashion passed, I put all of my confetti into a jam jar. You could still remove one with tweezers or a carefully dampened fingertip, a single bit for a decorative flourish on a Christmas card. I gave the jar to my mother, who had a taste for cast-off things.

Then one day I found her at her desk with tweezers over the whole glittering pile. She had six or seven orange medicine vials lined up before her and dropped each kind of confetti into its proper vial, all the stars alone in one, all the hearts in another. My father said something about the outrageous uselessness of it, the absurd amount of time it would take to finish. But of course my mother finished. And when she was done, she got back on her bed, a perfect sphinx, and returned to her games of solitaire.

One night I found her standing in the dining room and look-ing out one of the windows. It was dark. *Don't turn on the light!* she said. I stood beside her and looked out the window. Nothing was there. My mother pointed. *Look!* A car was parked in front of the Baldwins' house, two houses up the street. I could see the black silhouetted faces of two people.

They sat in the backseat, facing each other. The faces moved together until they touched. Then they separated again. Back together, and then apart. My mother was bursting.

———

During recess, I stepped up onto the retaining wall that separated the courtyard from the schoolyard. The bottom of the wall was brick, and we played dodgeball against it. The top of the wall was concrete, about six inches wide, topped with a chain-link fence that I clung to as I walked. The wall got higher as I walked from one end to the other, which was a full story off the ground.

I didn't get all the way to the end, though, because partway through my climb a few boys ran up to the wall, giggling, looking under my skirt. They could see the eyelet trim. They might have seen my underwear. I walked as quickly as I could back down to the low end of the wall. The fabric swished as if it wanted the boys to keep looking. I couldn't stop it.

Walking home in my skirt, I stopped at the north side of Weeks, a two-lane road with a yellow stripe painted down the middle. The crossing guard had a bouffant and moved her arms and legs quickly, like a helpful jointed toy. That day I held my chin up, my nose pointed skyward, as I crossed Weeks Road. I'd gotten the idea from a storybook. Fairy-tale people, before their comeuppance, walked with their chins up, proud and prim. I wanted to be the proud, bad girl who trod on a loaf. I wanted to challenge the world to break me. I wanted to explain that I was not yet broken.

———

One day, while Bee and I were walking home from school, a woman stepped out onto the sidewalk, holding a black camera. She said that she was in college, and that she was writing a project about friendship, and then she asked if she could take a picture of Bee and me. Bee immediately said yes and took my hand. The woman took our picture and then I shook Bee's soft hand out of my hand, and a few days later I mentioned to my mother that a woman had taken our picture near Weeks Road, right near the mustard-colored house. My mother became electrified, squawking that I couldn't just let people take pictures of me. Now, when I think about that day, I'm the woman, looking through her camera at me and Bee. Only Bee is smiling.

My mother scolded me exactly as she had when I'd told her about the men digging in the swamp, and then I understood that no one was safe to speak to, that my mother was the only adult in town who could protect me from what was out there, past the school and past the market and gas station, and past the edge of the woods that came right up to the back of our yard behind the house.

———

Before the snow fell and after it melted, we played four square. Bee always started in square A, Amber was B, I was C, and then whoever else wanted to play could be D, or line up and wait.

Regular rules included no double taps, no bubbling, and no side slams, corners, or treetops. Often the ball got close to the ground and we hit it fast, with topspin. The first person to miss the ball was out, and the players behind her moved counterclockwise in the big square.

In fourth grade we played hard. The fifth-grade girls played four square, too, but they didn't jeer at each other when they played, and they hit the ball gently from square to square. Their slowness seemed deliberate, as if they were danc-ing. Their skirts brushed slowly against their knees as they swayed. It wasn't so much that they looked different; they just looked as if they knew they were being watched.

———

When I was invited to dinner at Bee's house, my mother said I should bring something for Bee's mother. She and my father cast their eyes around the dim little den where we sat. Old books scavenged from the book swap, a vase picked up at some rummage sale. They couldn't conceive of buying a gift; a gift was something you gave away when you didn't want it anymore. I brought Bee's mother a book about the history of Waitsfield. It looked almost new.

Bee's mother called the tater tots *b'day-does,* and after I drank from my water glass, she immediately reached across the table and moved it, saying *Your glass belongs on the right side of your plate.* I ostentatiously picked up the glass again, took another sip, and put it back on the left. Neither of Bee's parents had gone to college, and her father worked construction. I can't remember a single thing about him.

Bee's mother inhaled above the scented candle in the middle of the table and murmured, *I wonder what this scent is,* exuding the satisfaction of knowing she had started exactly the right conversation. I carelessly said, *It's clove,* because it was one of the few spices I remembered from my mother's spice rack. Bee's mother took another whiff and looked across the table at me, uneasy. Somehow I had guessed right.

Bee's most prominent characteristics were that she wanted to be a newscaster when she grew up and that she hated the wallpaper in her room. It was an abstract brown and blue swirl, redolent of the late seventies. Bee told everyone she ever met that she hated her wallpaper. When I suggested getting a can of paint and covering the wallpaper with it, she looked terrified, but she wasn't scared of getting in trouble; she was scared of losing the second most interesting thing about herself.

In fourth grade all the girls were shown a movie that featured old-fashioned menstrual pads that were long and white and attached at each end to a thin white belt worn around the waist, under your shirt. The movie explained that we'd wash one belt while wearing a second belt. Why would you have to wash the belt? When would you know when it was time to change the pad? How did you carry a replacement pad around with you? The movie didn't explain that, but we all remembered the belts. After the movie our teacher explained that no one used the belts anymore, that pads stuck to your underwear now like fluffy tape.

Periods were still abstract to most of us. *So the blood squirts out, but you never know when it's coming?* Bee was terrified of that first world-rocking explosion. She said she would wear a pad every day, just in case. My mother wore something called Lightdays, which were like puffy stickers in the shape of your underwear and would probably suffice, but Bee wouldn't take such a chance. She was going to wear a full-on diaper every day, maybe starting tomorrow, just to be sure.

Bee liked to plan things, not because she had good ideas but because she enjoyed narrating. *First Barbie and Ken will meet on the beach, and then they'll go home and eat dinner on the patio, and then they'll bring the plates into the kitchen, and then they'll change into their pajamas, and then they'll have sex.*

So that's why people had Ken dolls! I was immediately be-witched. I had to see what the sex looked like, as stage-directed by Bee, and I couldn't bear waiting through all of the dutiful preliminary activities, so I suggested the couple skip their beach date. Then I suggested skipping the plate-clearing, and then I suggested skipping the changing of beachwear to pajamas, and then Bee looked at me slyly and said, like a knowing aunt, *Are you trying to get to something?*

I was so mortified at having shown my hand that I imme-diately suggested skipping the sex, too, so that afternoon the dolls never enjoyed physical union. I thought about it afterward. Would Ken lie stacked on top of Barbie, or would their only point of contact be their crotches as they bal-anced like acrobats?

———

After her parents built a greenhouse and installed a hot tub in it, Bee said she wanted to throw a birthday party for Charlie, the new girl. Charlie's birthday was two days after mine. *How do you think that makes me feel?* I said. I felt as if Bee had pushed me into the forest and run away and left me there. She hadn't remembered my birthday. Later she told me she wasn't going to throw the party, after all.

Then, weeks later, she invited me over. Surprise! It was a party—for Charlie and for me. She and some of the other girls had made cards and bought us new schoolbags. Mine was red and Charlie's was blue.

When we all changed clothes upstairs in Bee's room after soaking in the hot tub, we tried to hold our towels over ourselves. Bee's towel slipped, and everyone saw the tiny creased dumpling of her vulva.

Then we watched a movie on a rented VCR, as was the custom. The movie was a little dirty; two girls raced to lose their virginity by the end of summer. One girl was rich; the other was a townie, like us. We were still young enough that our physical boundaries were permeable; we braided each other's hair and knew the scents of each other's scalps.

The movie began to bore us, and someone to my left began tickling someone else. A few girls were giggling and wriggling. I kept braiding Charlie's hair, paying partial attention to the movie. The amount of background noise felt normal.

*You don't punch someone in the stomach!* Bee's father shouted. I looked over to where he was standing. A few girls were rolling about or pushing each other playfully, but I'd missed what had happened, if anything had happened. None of us would ever hurt someone on purpose, and my first thought was that the thing to do was not to react to his rage; I considered it as if from a great distance in space and time. No one responded as he stood there and steamed. My hands were still in Charlie's hair.

We weren't that young anymore, but Bee's father still let her sit on his lap like a child and pretend to drive his sports car. When he drove, he steered the wheel with just his thumbs, to show us that he could.

When I wore a hole in my new schoolbag, my mother took me to the notions area of the old dry goods store, and I chose a little yellow duck patch and sewed it on.

## 7

That spring I rode my green bike across the street to where the sidewalk started, in front of the Browns' house. Then I turned right and pedaled up the hill past all the other houses until the sidewalk ended. Then I clumsily turned the bike around and rode back down the hill and home. I knew that children were supposed to ride bikes for fun, and I dutifully played the part of a child having fun.

Sometimes I clipped my sneakers into my adjustable metal roller skates and skated up the hill to the end of the side- walk and then home again. Every few years, the Browns resurfaced their driveway and invited me to skate on it. It was smooth, and my wheels coasted quietly, without the teeth-rattling vibration of the street.

When the eye of a big storm passed over us, my father went outside. When he rejoined me and my mother in the basement, he said that Mrs. Brown had been outside, too, assessing damage, and had joked that they'd better go back inside quickly unless they wanted to see what it was like to fly.

For years afterward, my mother loved to tell people that Mrs. Brown had gone outside during the hurricane *because she wanted to fly,* her eyes wide open with contempt. She thought Mrs. Brown was crazy.

The neighbors at the end of the street had a gated chain-link fence that went all around their house. No one else had a fence like that. When they went on vacation, they hired me to pick up their mail and watch their house. I had a key to the chain-link fence. My main job was to check for broken windows. I opened the gate, walked all around the house, and locked the gate again. Then one day I saw a broken upstairs window. I called them and told them. I never heard another word about it.

An older couple lived on the other side of us. The husband had taught industrial arts at the high school: mechanical drawing, woodworking, and metalwork. The wife spent most of her time doing laundry. They didn't have a clothes dryer, and she hung the wash out to dry on a spindly structure in the backyard that looked like a big television antenna.

She washed the sheets every day and hung them outside on the whirligig. My mother said it was disgusting, but she didn't explain why.

Through the screens on their porch you could see two industrial spools set on their ends like tables in a giant's dollhouse. Sometimes I saw the couple sitting at them, facing each other, drinking from mugs.

One spring, the wife taught me how to pull weeds in the side yard between our houses, grasping them low and pulling slowly. I kept breaking the stems as I pulled the weeds, but the old lady didn't seem to mind. It was as if getting the weeds pulled weren't the point. It was as if our sitting together on the grass were the point. It felt good.

———

I was home alone one day when Amber knocked on the door and asked if I could come over and run through the sprinkler at her house. I ran upstairs and found my purple bathing suit and put it in the wire bike basket and started pedaling to Amber's. At the end of my street, my pedals stopped. A rubbery resistance. I called out, *Wait*.

The swimsuit was wrapped around the hub of the rear wheel.

We were half a block from Amber's house. Her father appeared. He moved slower than my father. He was short and his hair was pewter gray.

He told me not to worry. He took my bike and gently turned it upside down onto its handlebars and seat. I'd never seen anyone do that. He took a wrench out of his tool belt and removed the chain and my suit and handed it to me, and when I started to thank him, I choked. I hadn't known I was about to cry.

*You've done your good deed for the day, Papa,* Amber said brightly.

And the mechanic said, *That's why the good Lord put us on the earth, to help each other.*

His kindness was so potent, I could barely breathe.

Then we went inside. *Maybe my parents won't even find out what happened!* I said, scrubbing my swimsuit with hand soap in their little bathroom. Amber gently said that the grease probably wouldn't come off the suit. That's what she thought I was crying about.

————

Will, the boy I liked, helped one of the Special Ed kids line up the shot and push the ball into the air to arc down through the hoop. Over and over. He smiled and his eyes crinkled like an old person's. He was in fourth grade, like us, but he was as powerful as a teacher.

He and I walked next to each other, in a crowd, to the cafeteria one day, and laughed and sang the jingle to a television ad for a local chicken restaurant. A line had been crossed. I had been with him, in public. I wrote an anonymous note to him asking if he liked me. I hid it at home, in the cap of my deodorant stick.

We all liked him, my friends and I, all the tough girls from our side of the school zone, and one day someone said that Will liked me. *A dream come true,* a girl meanly added. I didn't know what to do. I couldn't look at Will anymore, so I didn't, not even one day in the hallway, in the same crowd, when he looked at me and seemed to want to speak. I stared straight ahead. I couldn't admit to the power of my desire. I had to figure it out in private first, before I could uncover it in public, but I never figured it out. I had no character to speak of, no loyalty to anything. I made fun of anyone, given the chance, just as my parents did at home, talking about me, talking about their closest friends.

———

When Bee, Amber, Charlie, and I formed a club, I wrote the club philosophy and rules and the code we would use to write each other notes, and when we voted for president,

Charlie won. We practiced spitting phlegm onto the school's chicken-wired windows, doing backflips off the playground equipment, and vaulting over the giant truck tire sunk halfway into the earth.

Charlie often brought candy to school. I held out my hands like a supplicant, and she tipped the box and let the candies fall into my hands. I couldn't believe how much she was giving me. Just giving it to me, when she could have eaten it herself. I poured the candy into a small pile in my desk, to the left of the groove that held my pencils. My textbooks sat in two neat stacks. Between the right-hand pile and the side of the desk I kept my plastic ruler, standing smartly on its edge. In the middle, between the piles, I kept my plastic protractor and metal compass.

I dipped into the candy every few seconds. It was raspberry-flavored, sweet and tart.

The substitute teacher said, *This one, popping candy into her mouth!* The girl in the front row turned around to look at the girl behind her, but it wasn't her. The girl in the second row turned around to look at the girl behind her, and that girl turned around to look at me. It had happened in such an orderly way, at once I knew exactly what to do. I turned around to look at the girl behind me. She was gazing straight ahead, like a cow.

———

The first time I went to Charlie's house, the housekeeper answered the door. I greeted her, but she just pointed her eyes at me and made me know that I was to follow her to the parlor. Charlie's mother behaved as if the housekeeper were an apparition.

During dinner with Charlie's family, Charlie's mother introduced me and said that my father was a doctor. I immediately corrected her, and she looked at me with a slight smile, as if I were telling a polite joke.

After dessert, while the ladies had tea, Charlie and I took her littlest sister upstairs to get ready for bed. Out of nowhere, the girl said, *Ruthie shouldn't have contradicted Mother in public*. I hadn't known that rule. There must have been others I'd been breaking all that time. I felt sick, and in my mind Charlie's mother took on monstrous proportions.

I adored Charlie, and I knew I'd never know her as well as I knew Amber and Bee. I don't know if I adored her because we'd never know each other very well, or whether my adoration had come first and hung a scrim between us that I'd always stay on the other side of, so I could keep seeing my own special version of her and keep adoring it.

———

A wholesale earring catalog arrived one summer. I sat on my bed and looked at the bright pictures on the blue pages.

Rainbow-striped hoops, small and fat. Heart-shaped studs in every color. Zebra stripes. I carefully marked the pages of my favorites, dog-earing and un-dog-earing them, assigning myself to choose my favorite twelve, favorite six, favorite three. I kept the catalog in the drawer of my night table. I never ordered any of the earrings; that was unheard of, to pay for something when I could enjoy just looking at a picture of it.

One day my mother asked me what color my eyes were. The bank teller had just said something about a cat's green eyes, and my mother had immediately said that her eyes were green, too. A cat's eyes were green; her eyes were green; what color were my eyes? If they were green, too, then the teller might congratulate my mother on having guessed right. She had no idea that a normal person would find it insane for a mother to ask her only child what color her eyes were.

But I sensed that she was also trying to see what it would be like to be that unattached to me. She was practicing, to see what it would be like to hurt me, a lot, to show how much she loved me. She had to be careful. If anyone found out that she loved me, we'd both be in trouble.

For a while I'd have to suffer, out in the open, the only girl without extra sneakers for gym class, but it was only because my mother's love was so much greater than all the other loves. It was that much more dangerous, so she had to love me in secret, absolutely unobserved by anyone, especially me.

# 8

My mother's aunt Rose and uncle Roger invited us out to dinner at a fancy restaurant in Boston for no reason at all. This was an unusual event for my parents and me, but not for them, apparently; they'd also invited a couple of friends. It was dizzying, thinking that this, too, was part of my life.

The restaurant had appeared on the Best of Boston list as the best French restaurant in the whole city. I'd read about it in *Boston* magazine, which my parents occasionally brought home from the dump.

The drive into the city felt slow, as if we were floating on a barge. There was traffic on the narrow old streets. The sun moved lower and the sky got darker and the buildings loomed tall, heightless, impassable, but I didn't feel trapped; I felt safe.

Then we walked through a door and an anteroom and into the main dining room, which had long cream-colored curtains and tablecloths and gold-rimmed plates. We sat at a big round table. My mother fidgeted with her hair, and her silver bangle bracelets clanked loudly. Rose and Roger and their friends were already there. Their friends were a couple, younger than my parents. The woman wore a thin sweater the color of butter and had long straight blond hair and an angular face so faceted that it looked like a vertebra. Her simple clothes were beautifully cut, her adornments so minor they seemed like almost nothing. A thin gold ring, a tiny gold pin. She was upper-class American and her husband was European, with olive skin and black hair, but dressed in the same quietly expensive way.

There was no water on the table, just cocktails and wine, and I was terribly thirsty. I didn't know what to do, so I whispered to my mother. She didn't know what to do, either. I kept eating my bread and butter. A waiter finally came to take the dinner order. Somehow I managed to ask him for a glass of water.

He brought the water almost immediately. The glass had a slice of lime in it. I picked up the glass and took a big gulp, and it was fizzy mineral water, bitter and salty, worse than no water at all. I swallowed the gassy mouthful and put the glass down, almost tearful. I whispered to my mother that it was mineral water, not real water, and she looked frightened.

Rose saw that I was about to cry, which made it even harder not to sob right there, but then some water appeared, and I drank it all and almost immediately needed to go to the ladies' room. I got up and a waiter appeared and told me where to go.

The bathroom door was tall and heavy, and the bathroom was for just one person. It took several steps just to get to the toilet, and I decided not to lock the door because it was already too much to occupy this bathroom in this restaurant where I didn't belong. I didn't deserve to use it. If someone had an emergency, they could come in. I sat on the toilet and started to piss, and then the door opened and a short waiter dashed in and started unbuttoning his black pants. *Excuse me,* I wheedled from my seat. No answer. *Excuse me.* The piped-in music was too loud. *Excuse me!* He looked terrified.

After that I walked back to the table and sat down as if nothing had happened.

After dinner it was decided that we would go to Rose and Roger's house, a short walk away. It had begun to drizzle, and outside the restaurant, uniformed men stood with big umbrellas, helping people out of their cars.

It was late. We walked in the streetlit dark. My shoes made an old-fashioned sound on the cobblestones.

Rose and Roger's newly decorated living room was cream-colored, like the restaurant. We all admired it. The younger couple were staying with Rose and Roger for the night. We all said goodbye. Then Rose opened the door and it was pouring rain.

Rose opened a closet and pulled out several coats. I was in awe of someone who would even own three raincoats, let alone lend them out to people she almost never saw, but at the same time I was thinking that maybe if Rose was so careless about her possessions I might get away with keeping one. My mother said, *These are Burberrys!* as if Rose were offering her a queen's crown. But Rose said it would be fine, that we could return them tomorrow, after it stopped raining. I looked at my mother. I knew that driving to Boston on two consecutive days would be impossible. My mother started to invent an excuse, but then Rose, understanding perfectly, said that they would come to Waitsfield and fetch the raincoats in the morning.

The coat was soft inside, and it was tailored. It had belonged to Rose's granddaughter. All the way home, wrapped in the coat, I pretended that we were rich.

———

The next day was Saturday. When I got up and went down-stairs for breakfast, a dozen corn muffins were sitting on the counter. *Don't touch those!* my mother said. They were for Rose and Roger, when they came for the raincoats.

I ate a piece of toast and honey for breakfast and then went back upstairs to read. At midday the doorbell rang. I heard unfamiliar voices. It was Rose and Roger and their friends from the night before. They came inside, smiling politely, and we all sat down in the living room. Our two sofas were blue velveteen, and the coffee table was stained dark brown, with cheap brass hardware. I saw it with new eyes now.

My mother got up and reappeared with a tray of corn muf-fins on saucers. We all took one. The European man com-plimented her so vigorously that she smiled helplessly. She looked like a schoolgirl who had just won a spelling bee. *These are from colonial America,* she said, slowly, as if the man might not understand. He didn't understand. *The PIL-grims,* she said. *In sixteen-twenty.*

He continued to praise the muffins. Why not make her feel as if she had won a contest? She gave him a note card with the recipe on it. She was glowing.

My mother brought up her triumph for years. *He was from Europe,* she'd say to anyone she could, opening her mouth wide for all the vowels. *He had probably never even HEARD of cornbread.*

She'd believed his praise was genuine. She hadn't noticed that he'd pegged her as a person who would snatch up any compliment into the maw of her unloved, throbbing little heart.

———

In the summer my mother drove the two of us to her parents' apartment complex, all bricks and concrete but for the parking lot, which was inexplicably cobblestoned. We signed in as guests.

The teenaged lifeguard crouched next to me at the edge of the blue pool, and there with my toes curled partway over the gray concrete lip, I'd flinch every time, jump instead of dive. It wasn't a problem with technique. It was a problem with fear, and she didn't know how to teach me not to be afraid.

I was afraid of continuing, afraid of finding myself somewhere I didn't have the skills or character or constitution to endure. Crouched there at the side of the pool, I stared into the bright blue depths. Something unendurable lay at the bottom of that pool.

The teenager set me up in the correct stance over and over. She didn't understand why it wasn't working. Again and again, not knowing how to dive past the fear, never getting it right, I was a slave to her determination. She had been parented too well, made into a perfect person, with plenty of energy to give to kids whose capacity to receive love had been diminished.

My mother wore terrycloth wraps over her swimsuit. Over mine, I wore giant T-shirts that came down past my hips. I wasn't naked underneath, but it looked as if I might be. One day my mother told me, seething, that my grandfather had said I had to stop walking around like that.

———

That was the last summer before middle school, and at the end of it my mother said that I would be getting new school shoes, slip-on shoes, because now I was old enough.

I stood in the shoe store while my mother looked around, and a shoe salesman asked, *Are you twelve?* and I said, *I'm eleven.* He got behind me and growled, *You're a tall eleven,* as if he'd caught me in a lie.

The store was filled with other women, some of them with their daughters. My mother didn't hear what the salesman said to me, but I knew that if she had heard it, she would have said something to let the man know that she and I were both grateful for his attention, and that we knew we were lifeless dolls just waiting for some man to breathe life into us.

9

Then it was sixth grade, and we all moved up to the middle school. Charlie was driven to school, and Amber and Bee and I started riding the bus.

Amber's niece went to school with us for part of that year. When she introduced herself to Bee she said, *I'm still thirteen. I know, I don't look it,* and the way she said it told us that she'd heard it so many times from so many men that it seemed as deeply a part of her as her own name. I remember there were so many horse chestnuts on the ground when she said it.

Amber had to go to school even when she was sick. In midwinter, with snow on the ground that had been accumulating and melting and reaccumulating, Amber watched me with devotional attention. When she coughed up a wad of bright green phlegm, I could see it behind her teeth. She waited for me to finish speaking before she turned away and spat the green lump into the snow. It fell through the lacy ice like a cannonball.

Amber and her niece smoked menthols in the mornings. Middle school started earlier than elementary school, and we had to catch the bus at seven-twenty, when it was still dark. The niece didn't trust anyone except Amber, and they stood aloof, several feet away. The niece sneered, *Don't look at me like that.* I said, *I'll look at you like I damn please.* I said it in my father's voice. Bee suggested that we walk one stop closer to the beginning of the route, and we did. Our bus took forever to get to school. It was the only bus that had to leave town to get us there. Everyone was tired.

———

The hallways at school were wide and dark gray, polished and worn. The floor curved to meet the walls like the base of an aqueduct. Everything was dark and shone, and the hall was filled with bodies in motion. Their loud voices echoed and overlapped.

And then a body hit another body hard, hit the front of me, and my teeth entered my soft lip, and I clamped my hand over my mouth.

Then I was swimming through the hall, my blood trailing me. The Latin teacher appeared, a gnome with eyes the size of dinner plates. *Are you all right?*

He wore thick glasses and tight clothes around his muscular little body, and he lived in a carriage house behind the school with his elderly mother.

I'd wanted to take Latin, but I couldn't. In school I needed to stay approximate. No one could know what I cared about. It would have been like driving in the country. You can't just go forty miles on the one state road and lie about where you're going, where you've been.

Bee sat at a cafeteria table with girls and boys. They all were in couples and seemed to swap partners constantly. Without ever speaking to any of them, I knew who was going out with whom. I watched them in the halls, and I listened.

I sat with some of the other girls from my elementary school until one day, when I sat down and they all got up and moved to another table. *There just isn't any room,* they said when I followed. It happened day after day until I gave up and sat at an empty table. In a few minutes, Charlie appeared, carrying her tray. She sat down across from me.

There was one table in the cafeteria where every girl was welcome. The girls in the remedial classes sat there, and the bullied girls, most of whom had a visible mark of difference, acne or birthmarks or a back brace, or they were dramatically overdeveloped or undersized. Looking at them sitting meekly together—I hated them for accepting their place. They chatted quietly and seemed grateful to have each other for company. I never sat with them.

That year Charlie made a clay box in art class. She glazed it in three colors. When she was done with it, she climbed up to the roof of the school and threw it down into the yard, where it shattered.

After school I walked home from the bus stop. When I turned the corner to our street, I could see my mother waiting at the front window. Sometimes she made a face at me with puffy lips. I had braces on my teeth and she wanted me to know that I wasn't fooling anyone, trying to close my mouth around them. She wanted me to know I was ugly. She was helping me get ready for the world.

———

In the morning I spat my cornflakes into a paper napkin and wadded it up and put it in my pocket to throw away at school. I remember being afraid to throw food away at home, but I also remember going upstairs to say goodbye to my mother on school days, so I must have eaten alone, guiltily. My mother croaked from her bed. My parents' breath and flatus collected in it all night and by the morning it stank.

Especially in the morning, I couldn't swallow food. If I were eating lunch or supper with my parents, especially at one of the bar-and-grills they liked, I could manage to eat a bite if I lifted a piece of fried potato off one of their plates. I couldn't eat from my own plate; a choking sensation would prevent it. As soon as my mother saw that I was eating, she moved some of her food to my plate, but as soon as it landed there it became inedible.

I think my bully chose me because he knew I wouldn't resist. Ryan O'Reilly spoke over the French teacher and said, *She sent Nick a holly-gram but he didn't send her one!* and the French teacher just ignored it. I pretended to ignore it, too, but Ryan knew that I was being corroded by shame, that I was becoming even more vulnerable, skinless.

I don't remember what else he said, but I remember it lasting minutes every class period, and that no one helped me. No one told him to shut up. His mouth hung open like a hot, stupid dog's. By then I was a nervous wreck, poorly nourished because I had such a hard time with food. *It's just nerves,* my mother said, meaning that it wasn't a medical problem, wasn't a real problem, was just something I'd have to endure, just as it was, just as I was.

I thought I'd die of it, but I didn't die. You can learn to eat violence. There is pleasure in not resisting. I dedicated myself to teaching my bully just how much a person can consume.

One day, waiting in line to ask the teacher something, I smelled sour milk. How strange, I thought, until I felt that the wet lump of my paper napkin had soaked through my pocket.

Late to science class, I saw Ryan on the back staircase to the science labs, rushing up as I was rushing down, and we were the only people there. I expected the most outrageous harm then, and got ready to absorb it, but when he didn't even look at me I felt disappointed. I wanted to bully him into hurting me; I didn't want to waste all that adrenaline. But then I saw the curve of his shoulders, as he dashed away into the history hall, and I could see that he was ashamed.

———

If you washed your hair in the shower before school and waited at the bus stop long enough, a thin layer of rime would form on the wet parts. On the bus the frost melted and the water evaporated. Our breath was thick and soupy in the air, and on the windows the condensation sometimes froze.

I washed my hair in the kitchen sink once a week or so, though there was no plan or pattern to it; no one had ever told me how often hair should be washed. I knew that some of the other girls at school took showers every morning, but my mother almost never washed hers, and she took baths, not showers.

I tried to ask the hairdresser, to whom my mother took me twice a year, if my hair was oily. I knew it was; before an appointment it was expected that I'd go an extra two or three days without shampooing, knowing that the haircut came with a free shampoo; it would have been foolish not to get our money's worth. The hairdresser said, softly and kindly, *You have a lot of oil.*

My hair still looked dirty after I washed it, and my mother and father never failed to tell me that I looked dirty, that when I washed my own hair it never looked the way it did after the shampoo girl washed it at the salon.

*You must be the only person in the world whose hair looks dirtier after you wash it,* my father crowed, my mother watching him approvingly.

My mother and I were once in the next town over, in the neighborhood where she'd grown up. We walked down the sidewalk, avoiding the ice, talking about a piece of clothing I'd just tried on in a shop. *Linda!* someone shouted. *Linda!* again, but closer. We turned around and saw a small, well-shaped man with thinning dark hair and a sallow but handsome face. He looked desperate, as if late for something. My mother said, *Oh, Anton!* It was the man who had cut her hair when she was a girl. The salon was still in the same storefront. He hadn't seen my mother in thirty years.

———

Just to the left of the crown of my head, I felt for a single coarse, curly hair, thicker and blacker than the surrounding hairs. I carefully pulled it out and looked at it. Sometimes the follicle itself came out, a tiny sheath of gray skin. I slid off the follicle with my nails and crushed it between my fingers. Sometimes the hair would come out with a bulb of rich black pigment at the tip. That pigment could be pressed into a sheet of white paper, maybe even smeared into a line. That darkness, from in me.

I pinched my eyebrows between my finger and thumb and pulled out seven or eight at once. I liked to count them. They were thin and pale.

Best of all was pulling out my eyelashes. They grew back quickly, and often I could tear one out and see its quivering pigment bulb. I stuck the lashes by their wet black tips onto the page of whatever book I was reading. On one page of *Little Women* I stuck five black-tipped lashes. That was a special day; I allowed myself only five lashes per day, since more than that would leave gaps that made people ask questions.

I felt a deep, specific itch. Only the sting of a torn-out hair could soothe that itch.

If anyone asked about my eyelashes I said that I rubbed my eyes and the lashes just fell out.

It seemed plausible. The sixth-grade classrooms were in the basement. That was the year that all of the girls' fingernails started peeling off in layers like mica. We peeled our own and each other's. It felt so good to force a nail between the layers of another nail.

———

Years earlier, after I'd fallen off my bike, my mother didn't change the bandage on my infected cut, and I had to swallow a penicillin capsule every six hours for two weeks. Inside the pink capsules the powder was acid green.

After I finished the antibiotics I developed a bumpy rash between my thighs. It came and went. The tiny round welts came to a head, like little blisters, and they itched. My mother gave me some cornstarch to put on it. One summer day, in the backyard, my father saw the rash on my thigh and asked, *What's that?*

My pediatrician, who practiced out of his skinny Victorian house, always asked if I got a lot of headaches or tummyaches, and I always said no, hoping to be found perfect.

Then one day, while we were trying on clothes in a discount store's fitting room, my mother noticed a lump on my hip. It was as if she'd made it grow on me, at that moment, with a silent curse breathed into the mirror in the tiny stall. I'd never seen the lump before.

I fought with my mother about it. She said it had to come off because it looked ugly. It was the size of a big marble. I'd have to have an operation, and then crutches. Off I went to the hospital. I slept over in the hospital the night before the procedure, and in the morning, a nurse gave me some brown liquid soap and told me to wash the area of the bump with it. The bump. It sounded almost cute. I lay down in my bed and then woke up and the lump-bump was gone and a big sticky white vinyl sheet was over my hip, with a lot of cotton gauze between me and it.

Maybe it needed to be removed from my hip and examined before we could know for sure that it wasn't malignant, but no one ever told me anything like that.

When I went back to school on crutches, my mother told me to tell the other kids that I'd hurt my leg. When Colleen Dooley walked up to me, I could see that she had been selected by a group of the curious to approach and ask. I said, *I hurt my leg.* Colleen looked at me with her sheep face and waited for me to say something else, but there was nothing else. She looked slightly disappointed, or sorry, or frightened. She backed away a little before turning around. It was in the basement hall, near the classroom where the teacher displayed cows' eyeballs in old mayonnaise jars. I could smell the formaldehyde seeping out from under the lids. It smelled sweet. Sometimes it got on my hands.

While I was on crutches I couldn't carry my schoolbag to my mother's car, so Colleen was enlisted to carry it for me. She worried that she would miss her bus. My mother never drove her home. Or did she? I remember only that Colleen helped me, and that after I was off crutches, I gave her a pink plastic charm for the sort of charm necklace we all wore that year.

Colleen and I sat next to each other in the front of the class-room. One day I felt angry at her and wanted to slap her, so I thought about it for a moment, and then I did. Then I waited for her to slap me back, and she did, and the transaction was complete.

While the wound on my hip was still healing, my mother smoothed the fresh white sheets over me, up to my chin, where the eyelet trim was folded down, and she smoothed the eyelet trim on the pillowcase. Then she stepped back and looked at me and the neat bed. She said in a quiet, awed voice, *You look like a bride.*

———

Soon afterward, I started getting migraine headaches at school. First I'd get the shimmering flash. It covered up one whole word on the blackboard, and then two words, and eventually it covered half my field of vision. After reaching its maximum size, the shimmer would fade at the same rate the pain bloomed in the other side of my head. Its borders were indistinct, like water. When the pain reached its maximum, I vomited. Then I felt better, just sleepy.

In English class, we were each given a mimeographed sheet of questions, a dictionary, and two class periods to look up all of the answers as fast as we could. I knew some of the answers without having to look them up, but I still felt terrified that I might not finish first.

On the second day of the race, I got a headache. It took a few minutes for the pain to reach its zenith, and then I vomited at my desk. I held the vomit in my mouth as I casually walked over to the sign-out log, wrote my name and the time, and took the bathroom pass. I opened the door and then closed it and walked across the hall to the water fountain and opened my mouth over it and watched the vomit slide down the five petal-shaped holes of the drain. I rinsed my mouth and spat a few times and went back to class and signed myself in and finished my sheet and won the contest.

———

One weekend morning I woke up and no one was home. I found a note on the kitchen table. *We had to go to the doctor,* it said. I took a bag of chips out of the snack cabinet and stood there for a while, eating them, and then I went up-stairs and got dressed. It wasn't often that I had the house to myself.

I went to my parents' room and pulled out the bentwood chair and sat at my mother's desk, a spindly one-drawer sewing table, one of the only places in the house that wasn't kept blank, empty, neutral, like a furniture showroom. I lifted up the blotter and found the creased, flattened letter from her old boyfriend and read it even though I already knew it by heart. *To beautiful Linda from the mountains, where it is easy to think of you . . .* Then I read the other things she kept there. There was a newspaper clipping: *Of all sad words of tongue or pen, the saddest these: "It might have been."* I opened the drawer and looked at all her paper clips and the little plastic box that held a roll of postage stamps. Then I shut the drawer and put everything back.

When my mother came home from the hospital the next day, she said she'd had a D and C. *To clean everything out,* she explained. I didn't know what she was talking about.

———

My mother picked at her fingernails every night, and when she didn't like the way she'd shaped them, she stabbed at her night table with the nail scissors. She painted her nails, too, sitting there in bed, and when she dragged the brush outside the line of the nail, she smeared the extra polish on the table. The table bore a scatter of pink and brown spots, and her black hair was everywhere, all over the carpet. If I dragged my fingers over it I could have made a hair ball as big as an orange. Her hair was thin and she was convinced that washing it made it fall out faster. You could see her scalp from across the room. And you could smell it.

That year all the girls started shaving their legs. My parents used blue plastic throwaway razors, and my father always had a red rash on his cheeks. He used the razors until they wouldn't cut anything anymore. My mother had a bumpy rash in her armpits.

When my own razor began to leave stubble on my legs, I asked for a new one. *What are you shaving with that?* my father screamed.

*You go through everything like it's nothing!* he said, sure that I was wantonly wasting valuable razors, and that I should have just let my pubic nest build and grow tall and fragrant, like my mother's reeking scalp.

———

I practiced the piano every day of the week, with a half page of my piano teacher's notes from our previous session and a short list of things to practice.

When I couldn't easily play difficult passages, I grunted and screamed and hit at the keys. When I did that, my mother called down from her bedroom, *Shuttup!*

One day, she called down the stairs, *That was a disgusting display of nothing!* She and my father were both up there.

My whole face was wet with tears. My nose ran. I could barely see the keys. Hating myself, hating my tears, I swiped my right hand under my nose and it came away streaked bright red with blood.

10

The dinner table at Aunt Rose and Uncle Roger's house was so long, I saw the opposite end of it foreshortened almost to a point. Our dinner plates lay under decorative plates with pictures on them. During the first part of the seder, we took turns reading the story of Passover. An aged uncle got up and hid the afikomen—a broken piece of matzo. The only other kid at the table was a cousin, who was older. After dinner, she and I got up to hunt for it.

The parlor—what a thing to see, a parlor! I felt like a member of the ruling class. It was two stories high, and on one wall hung a heavy antique mirror in a massive wooden frame. The cousin strode over to a sofa upholstered in peach-colored velvet and looked under a soft, round little pillow and brought up the afikomen in one hand. *We can say you found it,* she said briskly, and I didn't say anything and followed her back to the dining room. Before we reached the threshold she thrust the cracker into my hand. Then we sat down. *Ruthie found it!* I didn't say anything. If I moved my face my tears would run over.

After dessert we all went to the parlor. The cousin sat right down and played a simple jazz arrangement from sheet music already propped up on the piano. She sang a little. She played like someone playing music at a party, soft and secondary to the surrounding conversation. It was loose and casual and not all that good, I thought. Then it was my turn. I sat down and went inside myself so that I could only see and hear my hands on the keys, my foot on the damper pedal. Some of the people kept talking, and I heard someone shushing them. Then I was done, and when I got up from the stool and moved away from the instrument, Aunt Rose was staring at me. She turned to an old man standing next to her and said, *Abe would have loved her.* And the man nodded. *Abe would have loved you,* Aunt Rose said to me. She was talking about her father.

The big mirror loomed. The piano looked like a toy next to it, and so did the harp, which no one played. I touched its strings and plucked them a little. Aunt Rose said that she didn't know anyone who knew how to play it. If I'd lived there I would have played it every day.

———

I took a break from reading in bed on a Saturday morning and went to the bathroom and found a brownish smear in my underwear. I went to my mother's room, where she was reading in her bed, and said, *I got my period.*

She gave me a blue box of pads and then we both got dressed. To mark the occasion, she took me to a dark Polynesian restaurant with hula-girl murals and an illustrated menu of fruity cocktails. She had invited her mother, too. We ate plates of subgum and pork strips and fried rice. I sat on a cotton pad, bleeding into it, failing to understand why my grandmother would care about this gross, private milestone. She sat facing me, eating chow mein and wearing a small, proud smile.

We walked out of the restaurant, back into the light. I squinted. My mother bent over to pick something up. *I found a penny!* To her all pennies were lucky pennies, even if they were showing their tails, even if they lay in wet gutters. She thought she was the only one who saw them.

Everyone had somehow found out that Amber already had her period, so I told her about mine, but we kept it a secret. My mother must have overheard me on the phone with Amber and must have thought it was Bee, because when Bee came over one day soon afterward, my mother appeared, brandishing a giant box of pads. I was full of energy that needed to escape my body but couldn't. I ran, mortified, out of the room and upstairs, where Bee caught up to me.

She was soft, like a pillow or a pet. She gently glowed with understanding and let me know, silently, that my secret was safe.

My mother taped disapproving notes onto the bathroom mirror. *Rinse sink after spitting. Leave curtain in tub. Fold pads in thirds and put them in the trash; do not wrap them in Kleenex*—as I'd been doing, following the instruction from the movie I'd watched with all the other girls in fourth grade. We never spoke about it.

Then Bee got her period at school. She needed a pad and didn't have one. I always had a few mashed into a zippered pouch in my schoolbag. We made a plan to meet at her locker after homeroom, and standing there, facing the wall of metal doors, we conducted a magic trick: I reached into the pouch, took out two white pads the size of kittens, and handed them to Bee, and she put them into her schoolbag, and no one noticed.

In the backseat of Bee's mother's car, I speculated that a new pleated style of blue jeans was made to look as if you were wearing a pad and having a period. *No, that isn't it. Actually, there isn't anything like that,* Bee's mother carefully said.

The first heavy period I ever had was at camp, and I'd had no idea that a period was supposed to be so big; I'd thought it was just a smear, but no, it was something that had volume, that could spread, and I couldn't use a tampon because I didn't know where to put it, and I tried and tried while my friends cheered me on from the other side of the wooden stall door, but I couldn't do it, and so I couldn't go to swim class, and if you skipped swim you couldn't sail, and the sailing coach was a man, and I had to keep making up illnesses to explain why. *You should drink ginger tea!* he said, scandalized that someone my age wouldn't know that. *You need to get well! We need to get you back out on the water!*

———

Whenever we had a quiz, Colleen Dooley asked me what score I got, and I told her. Then she said the same thing, always: *Oh, that's so good.* Then she told me her grade, which was usually higher.

When she won an essay prize, the school held an assembly in the auditorium. She waited on a stool in the middle of the stage while we filed in and took our seats. In the cottony roar I knew I would never be heard, so I fixed my gaze upon her and, from ten or twenty rows back, made a thumbs-up sign. I pumped my thumb up and down in the air, and she didn't see me, but Ryan O'Reilly saw me. *Thumbs up!* he taunted, aping my gesture and saying it in a whiny voice. *Thumbs up!* I hadn't entered the contest.

A good person would have either been Colleen's friend or not; I was both and neither, couldn't choose. I hated myself for not being able to congratulate her, for not knowing if I should like her, not knowing if I liked her, not knowing why I was drawn to her, since she had no sense of humor or grace, but I knew surely that I deserved to be taunted, and I welcomed Ryan's reminder.

———

I didn't have to go to school if I had loose stools or felt nauseated, and I didn't have to go to the track meet if I couldn't convince my mother I really wanted to go. *Are you sure you want to do that?* she would ask, and I knew what to answer. I didn't have to go to any of the orchestra performances at school. I didn't have to go to any of the piano workshops, either; I just went to the recital unprepared and made many mistakes. Before I walked to the piano, I sat in the audience and counted the icy drips of armpit sweat that ran down my sides.

After a piano recital, the audience and the players filed out into the hallway, where on two folding tables sat a bowl of red punch, stacks of waxed paper cups, and plates of cookies.

The mothers took turns pouring the punch. One night, my mother poured, but instead of pouring and then handing a full cup to each thirsty child, she tried to pour punch from the big ladle into the cup while a child held it in his shaky little hand.

The red punch stained more than one pair of shirt cuffs that night. My mother just laughed. How funny it was! She glittered and shook like a rattle, there, behind the table.

———

That year I got a part in the school play.

The kids who were in all the plays and musicals were also in the cast, and I adored their confidence, which could be marshaled and concentrated in a thirty-second monologue and otherwise hung about them invisibly. If I stood close enough to one of them, I could feel their self-protective auras.

The auditorium was like the inside of a slaughtered animal, all oxblood paint and maroon velveteen. After the dress rehearsal, the star of the play gave a rousing speech to the cast as we stood around him. *It isn't a strong play this year,* he said, as if we'd all spoken about it, *but we're going to make the best of it and put on a good show.* It hadn't occurred to me that this could be the worst play the school had put on in years, but then I knew that it was.

In my first scene, alone on the stage, I silently got dressed for a dance. I stood and stared at a fixed point in front of me, as if looking in a mirror, and buttoned a shirt around myself. My internal monologue played from a recorded tape.

My second scene was a crowd scene, at the dance. One character asked everyone what time it was because she was afraid she wouldn't make her curfew. I remember her voice; when she sang, she opened her mouth wide and let her tongue rest against her lower lip.

My character was shy and unpopular. In the dance scene I wore a denim skirt and a baggy white sweater with silver thread knitted into it. I had never slow-danced with anyone before the dress rehearsal, but I knew what to do; I put my hands on the boy's shoulders and let him put his hands on my waist and we stood as far apart as we possibly could, in that position, and then sidestepped to the left together, then to the right, back and forth. I dimly recognized the song but wouldn't have been able to name it or sing along.

I was bathed in shame that this stupid play was my first slow dance, that it would live in my memory, the certainty that this boy didn't really like me, that he was ugly, and then someone snuck up behind me and took one of my partner's hands and put it squarely on my rear end. It stayed there for a moment, and then he moved it away.

In the opening scene, a spot shone on each of twenty or so characters, one by one, and each of us said one line. My line was *Everyone has a friend but me.*

A week or two passed. While I walked from one classroom to another, a girl shouted out behind me, *Everyone has a friend but me! And it's true!*

———

We all knew "Light as a Feather, Stiff as a Board," and we knew about Ouija boards, but those were things to do when there were more than two girls, and that night at Amber's house it was just me and Amber.

I took the candle and lit it and held the lit tip of it close to a dinner plate. I dripped the wax in the shape of an omega. Then I put my crystals around it—smooth rose quartz, amethyst, and hematite. The hematite had a crack in the top.

I was in love with Amber's older brother, not because of anything about him but because I was lit from the inside with a desire that fastened itself to any boy in the vicinity of my body. Monroe was a few years older than his sister, old enough to have come up from North Carolina with an accent he never quite shed, and a toothy smile.

Monroe never stood up straight; he was always tilting five or ten degrees to one side, like the anchor of a long suspension bridge. It made him seem taller. Monroe was old enough to remember the South, and his shiny gold hair seemed to retain the warmth of it.

Someday I would bring one of his wispy blond hairs home and tape it into my diary. Tonight, though, I was hoping he would materialize and see the waxy omega I had made and be impressed.

His room was upstairs, on the top floor of the house, and in fact he did appear, having smelled smoke.

*Put that out!* he said from the doorway. Then he came over and saw what was on the plate, my shiny stones, the omega now marred by drops of wax from the candle I'd stuck to the plate.

*Do you know what that means?* he asked, pointing at the melting omega, not impressed but scolding us as if we were naughty children. *That means . . . the end!* Monroe was just a regular person, after all. He didn't appreciate the nearness and power of the supernatural realm. My love for him cooled a little.

On weekends that I didn't sleep over at Amber's, I was so bored, I sat on the back steps blowing soap bubbles through a plastic wand. I taught myself to position the wand so I could blow hundreds of tiny bubbles or one big bubble. With my chewing gum I could blow a bubble inside a bubble. I could make a bracelet by tying hundreds of knots with some embroidery thread.

———

The seventh-grade science teacher kept a beaker of mercury on his desk. The first time he stuck his hand in it we were impressed, but it wasn't a lesson; it was a compulsion. He dredged his wedding ring in it until it came up steel gray. He poured the stuff onto the floor and picked it up with a sheet of yellow oaktag. When he dripped it onto his desk from a pipette, it bounced into tiny spheres as if it were reproducing.

That year our school bought a video recorder to be used for educational projects. The French and Spanish teachers had us act out little skits and then watch them. One day Mr. Science borrowed the video recorder and positioned it at his own desk, at the front of the room. He asked someone to come up and demonstrate how to light a Bunsen burner.

I hated being seen, and being filmed was even worse than being seen, so I'm not sure how I wound up behind the desk, facing the rest of the class, looking into the lens above which was a steadily shining little light. The class quieted and prepared to listen to what I was about to say. I picked up the box of matches and said, *This is how to light the burner*. I just kept taking another step, and then another.

I knew how to light a match, but I didn't know how to turn on the gas, or in what order I had to light the match, turn the handle, hold the match above the burner, kindle the flame, and adjust the gas supply and the air supply. Mr. Science had never shown us. He laughed, and then everyone laughed. I could have walked back to my desk and sat down, but I didn't. I knew that I had agreed to play a part, and I didn't know yet that I didn't have to comply. My shame fell from the ceiling like snow.

We were allowed to melt glass piping in the blue flame of a Bunsen burner and bend or fuse the tubes. Sometimes Mr. Science came to someone's station to blow a bubble into a molten glass tip. Then that person could use it to make a glass eighth note, one bubble and a bend. Mr. Science always told us not to touch the hot glass, but we still forgot sometimes and burned our hands.

———

I like to visit with the exhausted girl who once was me. I pick up the toddler and hold her until she is still. I stroke the little girl's hair. Now she is in middle school, and sometimes her father drives her to school. He leaves early, and she arrives forty minutes before anyone except the custodian, who pushes his long, flat broom of red and gray rags. She sits on the cold tiles, her back against a locker. Sometimes she sits in the Home Ec hall, sometimes Foreign Languages, where her homeroom is. Gray tiles, brown lockers with their fat shiny padlocks, the occasional corkboard. The ceiling is far away. She sits in the dark and waits.

I sit down next to her, waiting for the sun to rise, the buses to pull up, the lights to flick on, the lockers to open, the voices to echo in the hall where she has already been sitting half an hour. Her pockets are stuffed with paper napkins sodden with chewed-up and spit-out food she is too sad and frightened to swallow. She lets me stay there in the shining dark gray hall. She lets me wait there with her until it is time for her to get up and go to class.

The custodian passes the push broom over the worn concrete, always careful to avoid her feet, though it's just as likely that he doesn't see her, that she isn't even there. No one's there to watch her, so she just waits for the lights to turn on, waits to begin her performance. Once people start moving through the halls, carrying canvas bags heavy with books, she pretends she's just arrived, has been sitting there for just a minute or two, and she doesn't feel ashamed any-more.

My life felt unreal and I felt half-invested. I felt indistinct, like someone else's dream.

Once upon a time there was a house. It was brick on the sides and white in the front. It had a balcony and three porches and a Norway spruce in the backyard. Its address was 17 Emerson Road.

In 1907, right after their honeymoon, Winifred Cabot Fish and her husband moved in. Winifred was the only Cabot in her family who lived in a new house, built just for her, with her beloved husband's new money.

I imagined that by the time Winifred was old enough to marry, the Cabot money had been almost gone. She wasn't about to retreat to some summer cottage, so she married Mr. Fish and built a new house in town. This all happened in the twentieth century, but it might as well have happened in the seventeenth.

Mr. Fish knew as well as the rest of the town did that he was there to pay for the house and to preserve his wife's nobility. It was a privilege. Perhaps he even loved her, even though he was handsome and she had the broad hips and plain, weathered face of a woman who wears her name in lieu of beauty. Maybe her face was ruddy by then, having spent so much time outdoors; a woman like Winifred would not have painted her face.

Her sons were born and grew up and moved away, and then her husband died, and Winifred kept living in the house until she, too, finally died. The house stood empty for months while Winifred's last breaths floated out from around the drafty windows. Then, in the middle of seventh grade, my parents and I were invited inside.

The real estate agent's hair hung next to her face like a spaniel's ears, and her flesh billowed under her flimsy dress. She moved quickly, bending over farther than she needed to, barking out a theatrical laugh.

She stood too close to my father and flashed him her wine-stained teeth.

My mother said she knew why I didn't like the agent. *Ruthie doesn't like her because she's taking our old housie away,* she simpered. I was thirteen.

My father hugged my mother and she squawked like a child, wrinkled her face, and tried to escape his grasp.

After I went to bed I could hear my parents talking downstairs; they never did figure out how sound traveled in houses. My father said, *I'm not going to be involved with anyone other than my wife.* I didn't care one way or the other; the agent thought my mother was stupid, and my mother thought that I was stupid. I think she thought that I wasn't even real.

The house was cheap, maybe because Winifred had died in it, and the family had wanted to off-load it quickly. My parents sold our old house for three times the amount of what was left on the mortgage, and suddenly we were no longer house-poor.

Not just that, but our new house was in the second-best school zone in town and had once belonged to a grand lady. She had built the house, lived in it for eighty years, raised two sons, and died in the parlor, and I imagined her so completely that she became real. It wasn't a haunted house, but Winifred was there with us nonetheless.

———

From the outside, the small second-floor windows made our new house look as if it were squinting. I hated those windows and I hated the house with its little piggy eyes and low forehead. It didn't look anything like the long white faces of those who had lived in the neighborhood hundreds of years earlier. It looked like us.

Our front lawn was separated from the sidewalk by a stone wall about a foot high. My mother squawked at the children who walked on it. She said she worried they would fall and get hurt, but really she was territorial, like an animal.

Before the movers brought our things, I roamed the empty rooms looking for signs of Winifred. Small pewter sconces hung in each room. From the ceiling of the porch hung an old ship's lantern.

On the third floor there was a bedroom with a pale green carpet, a lavatory, and a small latched door that led to the attic. A pull-chain dangled from the attic ceiling, and I pulled it, and a bare bulb lit.

The attic was big and gabled and mostly empty. Boxes and bags were strewn around, all marked with the names of expensive department stores. I felt along the exposed beams and found some curled photographic negatives as big as postcards and held them up to the light. I saw a woman and a man standing against a tall tree. Their clothes look antique. In one shot, they stand in a tight embrace. It could have been Winifred and her husband, or it could have been her parents, or it could have been anyone.

The third floor already felt like a secret, extra space, and the attic was the most secret part of it, but the attic itself had an even smaller door in its wall that led to a crawl space. I crouched and crept inside, leaving the door open to let in the dim light.

The crawl space was half the length of the house. The outer wall was lined with faded pink insulation, and on the floor were old bits and pieces of wood. The dust on the floor was thick. About halfway inside, I came to a small pile of clothes—pants, men's underwear, and a shirt. They were stained red-brown all over.

The clothes felt like the green clay at the bottom of a floral arrangement that disintegrated in my hands. I brought them downstairs and showed them to my mother. *Blood,* she said. For a few moments she handled them in silent awe. Then she took them and threw them away.

It would take only a few years for her to question and then contradict my memory of them, of the word *blood,* and of the fact she'd even seen them. I must have imagined the whole thing. After all, to her, I was just a child.

I printed Winifred's negatives in the darkroom at school. The pictures show two pale people with dark hair. The woman's dress is bisected by a column of tiny, covered buttons. The people are young and neatly dressed. In one picture they are kissing in front of a tree trunk.

There must have been strands of her hair in the house when we moved into it, parts of her actual body, particulate and hidden. I could have been more careful, really looked around, peeked under the carpet at the corners of the rooms, swiped my fingers around the insides of the light fixtures, dug into the soil of the backyard.

Winifred and I walked on the same floors, turned the same lamps on and off. In winter she was cold. In summer she was hot, used the sleeping porch, looked out at the old Norway spruce in the yard.

When I remember the yard of the new house, I remember it in shade, in late afternoon, early autumn. I remember the whole town that way.

————

We were taught that the town of Waitsfield began in the early seventeenth century, with the first English settlers. The land's so-called Indians were part of the environment, like cranberries and corn. In the middle of the seventeenth century, the settlers' children bought the land from a local chief for five pounds of silver, and a colonial town was established.

In the next century, that town split in two, and then in the nineteenth century, a hundred years after the Revolution, one of those halves split again. Most of the land in the western part was owned by the Emersons, who donated and built the town hall, the library, two schools, and many acres of parkland. They named the town Waitsfield after their estate back in England.

When we moved to Emerson Road we continued to pronounce the *r,* as everyone did except the descendants of the founding families, who all said *Emmah-son.* My parents hired a boy to paint the side of the house, and he was an Emerson, and we said his name the way he said it, but we continued not to use that pronunciation for the street or the school, for to do so would have been pretentious, above our station.

The Emerson boy was on a break from boarding school. The rumor was that it had been his grades, but his grades were irrelevant. He possessed the kind of authority you can just say your name and have.

*The Emerson boy,* we called him. I don't remember his given name. He wore his overalls and red bandanna like a costume. At the end of the summer, after he returned to boarding school, my mother hired a real painter to redo the job.

Next door to us lived the Lowells. They'd been there a long time, and they were old and of the second-best family, per the old rhyme: *And here is dear old Boston, the home of the bean and the cod, where Lowells speak only to Cabots, and Cabots speak only to God.* Like good children, my parents and I spoke to the Lowells only when spoken to. They were too important to interrupt. I would never go inside their house, but I imagined the walls bore three-hundred-year-old portraits of their Massachusetts Bay Colony ancestors.

The Lowells kept a fat orange cat who sunned herself at our house, just outside the porch that my mother called the *conservatory*. I petted her soft underside. The cat had belonged to the Lowell girl and spent its nights at the Lowells' house. My mother resented the cat. She found it superior.

Next door to the Fishes, the Lowells had raised their girl and their boy. The children were polite. They took ballroom dancing with the rest of the boys and girls who went to private school and had small noses and straight teeth, girls whose hips would widen whether they continued riding horses or not, whose faces would tan and wrinkle from sailing off the Vineyard in summer, or, if they were especially good girls, Nantucket.

By the time he was ten the Lowell boy had learned to carry the weight of apologetic superiority. It would have been untoward to be seen striving in school. It was appropriate to strive on the cross-country team, or while rescuing a little boy from drowning in the pond once, in late summer.

———

Weak men who fall into positions of power are dying to give it up to anyone who will take it. The poor player would throw the ball to someone on the other team just to be rid of the worry of what to do with it, of the dread that he would have to be a man of action for a moment.

I imagined that Winifred's husband was handsome, dark in a way that none of the boarding school boys were. Mr. Fish thinks he'll become more powerful by proximity to Winifred. But these families, the long-kept bloc, are impermeable by mere marriage.

Winifred's mother takes out the social register, the blue book, and says, *Whom will I take to lunch today?* in front of Winifred's mother-in-law, who doesn't notice.

Winifred wouldn't have minded people seeing what she looked like without a wash-and-set. Beauty was for the lower classes, who needed it. Anyway, her hair dried smoothly, all by itself. She knew her stocky Mayflower ancestors had given her an inviolable standing in this small place. They had given her short thumbs and stubby fingers. She knew what wouldn't change.

When Winifred asked Mrs. Lowell if their boy could come to paint the doors of her house, Mrs. Lowell said that he would do it. The boy came on a Saturday morning.

Winifred looked at the Lowell boy. There might have been some warmth coming from the crown of his head. He was seventeen now. Winifred didn't offer him anything to eat; he wouldn't have accepted it. He was there to work, to paint the Cabot woman's Fish doors. The silence in the house seemed muffled, anticipatory, as if the building, too, were waiting for something to begin.

*Here, you can wear these,* she said to the boy, holding the clothes out to him. He went into the little downstairs lavatory to change. He left his clothes on the toilet tank, neatly folded.

What did Winifred do while the Lowell boy painted the doors? Did she busy herself with something inside, trusting that the boy would call to her when he was done? Did she find a corner of the sleeping porch where she wouldn't be seen, and watch the Lowell boy at his task? Did she walk up to the empty third-floor suite and wait?

The Lowell boy kept his face composed. His hair was almost white in the sun. When he finished his work he went back into the house.

## 12

I like to think that Winifred walked along the brook path in all kinds of weather, and that she in turn liked to think about the Lowell boy who had lived next door, twenty years older than her little ones. He came home from college for the summer and mowed the lawn and sweated round stains under his arms. The stains looked clean, like pure brook water.

Winifred daydreamed while she stitched a patch onto a pair of pants that would soon be outgrown, and then she used her mother's old seam ripper to tear out the tiny stitches and save the patch in case the boy needed it again, and he would never need it again, but Winifred kept it, and when she was dead and the others were sorting out her last remaining possessions, they found the soft little patch and smiled condescendingly at her mother-love, and they threw the patch away, not suspecting at all that while she sewed it onto the little torn knee of the little pants, long gone to threads, her heart beat a hard pulse while she thought of undressing, tenderly, almost as she would undress her own tiny sons, the neighbor boy. Tasting in her dream his softness, just slightly salty, slightly sour, barely any hair, barely any scent, the sweet rank sweat underneath, the spice of it, the boy arching his back a little and dropping into his own dream.

I bet Winifred thought about the Lowell boy all day while her sons were at school. I bet Winifred wanted to tell the Lowell boy, had planned to make him her confessor. I bet he was the one, of all the Lowells and Emersons and Thayers in the neighborhood, that she chose. His white eyelashes, his lean arms, brown from being on sailboats all summer.

When Bee came over, I showed her the photographs I'd printed and told her my theory about Winifred and the Lowell boy. Bee looked confused. Then, in her creaky voice, she asked, *Why do you think that when you've never met either of them?* Clearly she needed to brush up on her Greek mythology. The story of Endymion and Selene is exactly like the story of a Cabot woman and a Lowell boy, I tried to explain. But Bee didn't know the difference between a Cabot and a Lowell or even the difference between Amber and Charlie, and I didn't have the heart to teach her.

———

When Winifred's boys were grown and gone, she and Mr. Fish took a cruise.

Winifred came back, and Mr. Fish didn't, and Mrs. Lowell didn't ask. She lived next door to a Cabot now, and a Lowell didn't have the right. The leading between the panes in the conservatory slowly dulled, and the flagstones on the front walk faded. Everything else stayed the same.

Mr. Fish's obituary ran in the *Courier. Died suddenly while en route to Norway,* it read. He was buried in Boston, among twelve generations of Cabots at Granary Burying Ground, quite an achievement for a Fish.

I wanted to know how he died, what Winifred did when she reached Norway, and how she told her sons, who would have been in their thirties, but the listing was formal, gnomic, abbreviated. *Private services were held. Rev. Townsend Brooks officiated. Survivors include his wife, Winifred (Cabot) of 17 Emerson Road, and two sons.*

Everyone paid their respects to Winifred. No one asked any questions about it. Everyone assumed Winifred had a closer friend to tell the story to. That it would come out, someday, but it never did.

I imagined that Winifred spent more time at home after that, needlepointing. She and her friends sold pillow shams to each other to raise money for the library and the horticultural society. Winifred's stitches were so tight that they looked painted on.

My mother had found something, too, in our new house: a locked cabinet in the corner of the cellar, near the oil burner. We took the door off the hinges. The cabinet was full of bottles. My mother liked to say that Winifred had had a husband who drank, but my mother thought all Gentiles drank. I thought about Mr. Fish falling off the upper deck of the ship, blotto.

Or perhaps a vessel burst, and that would explain the blood. Winifred could have brought the bloody clothes home as a memento mori. Her widowhood was incorruptible. What a testament to enduring love, to love that even death cannot dissever.

I tried to imagine Winifred with a broken bottle in her hand. I tried to imagine her shoving Mr. Fish over the side of the ship. I tried to imagine her shooting him with a little pistol. And it was only after I imagined every violent thing she could do to him that I imagined him jumping over the side of the ship into the cold water. And I thought I understood how Winifred could come home and be alone for the rest of her life.

I didn't talk to anyone about Mr. Fish because I wanted the story all for myself. I didn't even try to imagine it happening in a certain part of the ship or at a certain time of day. I didn't think about whether other people were there, witnesses or resisters or accomplices. I wanted to keep the details mysterious so that no one could contradict them and take them away, lift them like a photograph out of a scrapbook, leaving only its shadow on the faded page.

I thought about her, all alone in her house with her wallpapers and her pricklings of guilt, a small pile of clothes in the little crawl space upstairs, just for her.

The clothes and the photographs I'd found in the attic didn't add up to a murder, but I wanted to believe that Winifred was a murderess because I wanted to have such power myself someday. I barely spoke, but my power was building up in me. I stockpiled it in silence.

But it was paint on the clothes, not blood. Winifred stored the clothes in the crawl space and visited them on the maid's days off. She lay on a chaise in the tidy attic with the dirty clothes over her face. It was as if the Lowell boy were there again. I wonder how many times they touched in life. I wonder how he would remember her now.

Even after the clothes took on the wet smell of a Massachusetts attic, Winifred remembered the old whiff of sweat in them. The memory was enough.

———

Charlie looked at the picture of the two people kissing. I told her that Winifred might have had an affair with the Lowell boy. She said, *This isn't a boy. Why do you think that?*—Because . . . *Cabots and Lowells,* I started to say.—*You know not all Lowells are upper-class,* she said. *Some of them are swamp Yankees.* What? *People with good names but no money like the Lodge boys who live by the brook.* I'd never distinguished them from Anna Lodge, who lived across town in the estates, but Charlie did.

That night I thought about the ancient Lowells next door. Were they swamp Yankees? The only swamp I'd ever seen was back across town, where Amber and I had watched the men dig a hole. I couldn't imagine any connection between that swamp and these elderly neighbors.

Maybe the Fishes had gone to the Lowells' Christmas party. Maybe the Lowell boy easily shook hands with each guest, but when Winifred, last in line, stood before him, he froze in place, his arms hanging. Etiquette demanded he take her hand; etiquette forbade him from touching the object of his desperate outpourings. Those two ideas got confused in his head. He stood still in the yellow-lit hall. Winifred told him good night, not looking at his face, and left.

She knew that the best way to keep a fire burning is to feed it, but not too much. An old, slow fire is best. Old fires in old houses.

I didn't care about what had happened to Mr. Fish. I cared about what had happened to Winifred, though, in that house that was like a prison upstairs, with its little prison windows. The doors were dark red, like the blood beating between her thighs as she looked out over the magnolia between her house and the Lowells'. She held her legs tight around it, protecting it.

Winifred might have wanted to touch the Lowell boy, but she lived a long time. People who live that long aren't impulsive. They protect a little ember and stay just a little bit too cold all their lives. The clothes were tossed up into the crawl space, maybe, before a party, or before a guest was coming to stay in the upstairs suite, or maybe the Lowell boy never even wore them. Maybe Winifred never even went into the crawl space. My mother never did. Maybe it was just the builders, in 1907, and then me.

Winifred died in the house, as women of her station do, in the dining room, attended by her sons and nurses. But before that, something happened, and not one other person knew it, and she enjoyed thinking about it in the dining room, in that bed, attended but alone, enjoyed not having to talk or even to acknowledge the others, at last, not obliged to get up from the dining room table, able to lie abed in that room that had seen so many dutiful servings of steaks and drinks and yellow sponge cakes. She had been there for all of them; they were her life's minutes and hours. In that bliss of paralysis and pain inaccessible, the morphine curtain drawn all the way across it, she spent the end of her life.

Winifred was a hundred and two when she died. The house was only eighty, but it kept getting older.

## 13

Early in the morning, before school, I sat and read and waited until it was time to leave on foot. One day the phone rang and I picked it up. *I'm so lonely,* my long-ago-widowed paternal grandmother said. *Can you come over and visit?* I told her that I had to go to school. *Oh, school . . .* she said, trailing off, remembering my age. I guess I could have called a cab.

She was already demented by then. She sat in her house, on her impeccably maintained sofas flecked with gold thread, looking at her barrel-shaped stained-glass lamps that hung from white plastic chains. Her refrigerator doors were full of bottles of pink nail polish.

We didn't visit her anymore. No one ever explained why, but I think it was to protect ourselves from witnessing the horror of her decay. Or maybe now that her memory was burning away, my mother reasoned that she wouldn't remember our visits, so it wasn't worth doing if we weren't getting credit for it.

When my grandmother was moved from her house to a nursing home, I was never brought to visit her, but my parents brought me along every weekend to clear out her house. It should have taken a single day, but my parents were doing it themselves, piecemeal, as if it were a game, as if priceless treasure were somewhere in a drawer with a false bottom, and they pored over every trinket, every gas-station glass. None of the boxes of photographs were labeled, so they all got thrown away.

I complained bitterly that I wanted to skip a day, or even just an afternoon, to spend time at Bee's house, but my parents were furious that I would even ask. Their fury was the fury that my grandmother had inconvenienced them by getting sick, or that she had cheated them by leaving nothing of value for us to find in her attic or her jewelry box.

She finally died on a day that I had a volleyball game, a home game. I walked home for a snack before returning to school for the pregame practice. My father was home and had put on a suit, two highly unusual things. I could tell from the context that my grandmother had died, but my parents didn't tell me until I got home from the game. When they told me, I said, *I know.*

My parents brought home her giant green bottle of even greener Prell shampoo. It sat on the corner of the tub. She had diluted it. It lasted forever.

———

I was sixteen when I gave a solo piano recital at my music school's concert hall. I wore a brown and black knit dress with a long skirt. It came from a cheap store, on sale.

The other students at the conservatory had beautiful invitation cards made for their solo recitals, printed on cream-colored card stock with their names and maybe a tiny illustration of a piano. They were so elegant, so adult.

I asked my mother for some invitations like those, but instead she bought a pack of invitations from the card store, for a child's birthday party, in the shape of a piano. On the keys were printed letters spelling out *Something Grand Is Being Planned!*

It didn't occur to me that I could have figured out how to get the invitations made myself. Instead I took the shame and packed it into my body along with all the shame that had come before. It was my birthright.

I thought my mother did these things specifically to shame me, to spread pain. It never occurred to me that we might have had a little money, by that point, but we didn't know yet how not to be poor.

I shined my lace-up boots carefully. The background of my life was white and angry, with violent weather. It was considered a sign of character to swim outside in September, and I did that. By then Amber was taking remedial classes and had a different lunch period, and I barely saw her anymore. Of my two remaining friends, Charlie and Bee, only one would survive high school.

After Charlie's parents divorced, her mother remarried an older man. Charlie's new house was a few blocks away from mine, a big Victorian with a deep front porch and a plaque. Her room was at the top, and it had a window seat with a cushion she had sewn.

Charlie went to parties with all the handsome boys I liked. She sewed herself a cape with darts and grosgrain edging. She walked slowly, with sad grace. She said to me, point-blank, *I don't dress for myself; I dress for boys.* I barely knew how to dress for myself at that point, having put all clothing and even the idea of fashion in my blind spot and kept it there.

She babysat and asked the fathers to drop her off at parties afterward, never at home. After she woke up in a strange place, bleeding, she paid for her own psychiatrist. She tried to get me to come to parties. She already knew so much more than I ever would. She knew that her mother was *having affairs,* she said. Her stepfather didn't know it yet.

Sometimes Charlie threw her hair over the side of the tub, and her mother washed it for her. She never rubbed her hair when it was wet for fear that it would break. It fell down her back as thick as a mare's tail, heavy and straight. Sometimes, when her hair was a little dirty, she put it up in a bun with nothing holding it but a hat pin.

I always did the homework, but Charlie only did it sometimes. When she was asked to stand in front of the class and summarize something she hadn't read, someone whispered, *She doesn't know what she's talking about!* and Charlie casually said, *Perrr-ceptive!*

In our middle school yearbook, she looks ageless. Her hairline is high and her hair is light. She has no eyelashes and almost no eyebrows. In my copy, she colored in her nostrils in black pen. She wrote, *Did you ever fix Colleen's French book? Well, I hope I see you again sometime soon.*

She was referring to the time in seventh grade when Colleen had snubbed me by inviting every girl in homeroom but me to her birthday party, and I thought I'd get even with her by whiting out all of the page numbers in her French book.

I remember telling Charlie about it. She listened so patiently. I never worried that I was boring her.

She was a drinker, but I found that out only after she confessed that her mother had found, hidden in her dresser drawer, a shampoo bottle filled with vodka and a miniature mouthwash bottle filled with sambuca. One of the bottles had leaked.

———

I still went home with Bee after school sometimes. We cooked noodles for her little brother when her mother worked late at the hospital.

One day Bee passed me a note in study hall. She had gone to a boy's house after school. *Someone bit the big one yesterday, but a milkshake came out instead of pee!*

My mother must have gone through my bag; that night she screamed at me. *What does this mean?* I had no idea. I wasn't scared or even worried because I didn't know I'd been entrusted with a secret. I was the perfect confessor.

Then my father joined in. I watched them as if I were watching a play, two angry people screaming at someone.

My mother opened her mouth wide when she was screaming. She must have gone through my bag every day.

The next time Bee came over after school, my mother asked her what her chores were, and Bee said she had to clean the downstairs bathroom. It was a little lavatory separated from the kitchen by swinging doors that didn't completely close.

*How do you clean it?* my mother asked.—*I clean the sink, mop the floor . . .* she started. Then, in a different voice, she said, smiling a strange smile, as if it were a joke, but she wasn't sure who the joke was on, *clean the toilet. . . .*

Bee told me that, alone at home one day, she had poured herself a glass of wine and drunk it. *Then I threw the glass into the fireplace,* she said. I wondered where she'd gotten the idea. She added she'd swept up the glass and put it in a paper grocery bag and thrown it away. She told me those things while I was still wondering where she'd gotten the idea in the first place, so I didn't notice that she was testing me to see whether I'd understand. She was telling me that she'd absorbed so much of her father's violent attentions that she had to get it out of herself, to inflict it on a mute, inanimate object that would never tell.

In ninth grade Bee came to school with a gauze-wrapped hand. *I broke a thermometer and tried to drink the mercury,* she said to me, *but I spilled it, so I just used the glass to cut my hand.* I didn't know what to say. I didn't say anything. It seemed like a joke. It seemed like something that Mr. Science might have tried, just one quivering silver orb, rolling around on his tongue while we all squealed.

Bee held out a puffy, bandaged hand, her consolation prize for dropping the precious poison. Her eyes were wide and watery. I didn't know what to say; I'd have been just as baffled if she'd come in clutching the leash of an exotic animal and said, *This is what I need to keep with me now.* I wish I'd said something, though.

By high school Bee had developed a Boston accent and started teasing her hair. We still greeted each other warmly in the hall but we didn't otherwise cross paths.

A few months before graduation I saw her in the hallway, hugely pregnant, her navel jutting out like a bottle cap.

I met her eyes then, after I saw her big belly. She looked at me and in that look she reminded me that years ago, I had failed to understand her suffering. In that look she let me know that she had done her best to keep me in her life. But she looked hopeful, too, that her father wouldn't want to go near her anymore. I hope she was right about that.

## 14

On the day of Uncle Roger's birthday party, my mother started getting dressed at ten in the morning, hours before we needed to leave. She stood in her underwear and looked at herself in the bowed full-length mirror on the bathroom door. *Disgusting,* she said.

*And what piece of shit are you going to wear?* she said to my father. He went to his closet and picked out a pair of tan pants. My mother called them *wash pants,* as opposed to woolen pants that needed to go to the cleaners. He took a shirt from his drawer and put it on.

My mother said that he should wear a suit.

My father undressed to his white T-shirt and rumpled white boxer shorts. He put on his blue suit. *Disgusting!* my mother said. *Why can't you stand up straight? You're too fat for those pants.*

I wasn't going to get dressed until five minutes before four, and after I did, my mother looked at me. *You need a girdle for that skirt to hang right.* I didn't have a girdle.

Then I realized that I was about to vomit.

*I can't go,* I said, and sat down. My voice sounded as surprised and confused as I felt. The only thing that could prevent me from throwing up was the assurance that we wouldn't go to Roger and Rose's house that afternoon. The reasoning seemed insane, but the thought came to me fully formed, as if sent from an oracle. I believed it.

My mother went upstairs without saying anything, and when she reappeared she was holding out her hand, palm up. There was a small white pill on it. I took the pill and put it in my mouth and someone gave me a glass of water and I drank it down. Then my father drove us to Uncle Roger and Aunt Rose's house.

———

The door was opened by someone we didn't know, who led us into a big room. A caterer in a black jacket offered us drinks. Another brought a plate of snacks. By then the little white pill had worked its magic, and I was feeling friendly and congenial. I joined a conversation with some much older people without my usual fear that they'd find out I had no idea what to say to them, or to anyone. In my peripheral vision I looked at their grayish teeth and drooping skin while they talked. I smiled at them as if I weren't thinking about the hairs in their ears.

My mother was sitting in a corner with her sister. How did they manage to find two chairs in a corner? They had dragged the chairs into the corner from some other part of the room. They were both holding plates on their laps that were comically full of food. They had emptied an entire tray of tiny quiches and were eating them with their hands. They weren't speaking or looking at each other or at anything but their food.

A small boy pulled at my clothes. His sweater looked like cashmere.

He wanted me to follow him across the room. He dropped to the ground and crawled under the piano. I followed him. I was such a good guest; I could even tolerate children. Now we were both under the piano. My legs were folded awkwardly so I wouldn't flash the crotch of my underwear. I could see my mother watching me from her corner.

Then someone made the clinking-glass sound. It took a long time for everyone to be quiet at the same time. Then someone said that Uncle Roger was ninety years old, and we all clapped our hands and smiled. I was smiling appropriately, as if I were thinking about only one thing at once, one feeling at a time. I was happy. Then I was letting my eyes tear a little. I lifted my glass and took a sip.

When we got home, my mother carefully said to me, *Your father thought you looked nice this time.*

———

Back then it would have sounded extremist, paranoid, delusional, to say that all attention to girls was tinged with sex. Even now it seems almost unbelievable. And so when the gym teacher put his hand on my ass, moved it around as if trying to get the dimensions of it, to quickly memorize its shape in the full light of the gym, forty other kids and teachers milling around, doing their thing, I thought, How old-fashioned and almost tender, this so-called molestation. I understood that it was wrong, but, after my first thought, which was that maybe this is normal, I found it sweet. I knew that, on some level, he liked me.

When I graduated from middle school, he wrote in my yearbook, *You remind me of the caterpillar who becomes a butterfly.*

When I started high school I tried out for the volleyball team, for which he was the coach. I had my period the whole week of preseason. I did the drills and bled into the cotton batting inside my shorts. I could smell the gore.

When the coach said to us that we needed to focus on what was happening in our peripheral field of vision, I said that I didn't have peripheral vision. I didn't believe that my eyes could be that clever.

He asked me to stay after practice, and when we were the only two people left in the gym, he had me stand at the net and stare forward. Then he bounced a ball past me, on the right. Could I see it? I could.

I felt it: someone was taking care of me. But he never touched me again.

## 15

I had no idea how to take care of a child, but I was in high school, and that was good enough for the family at the end of the street. I babysat their two little boys. They were two and four years old.

The father's pale eyebrows were almost white. He seldom spoke. Even though it was a short walk home to my house, he drove me, and before he turned the car on, while I sat in the passenger seat, he silently made a wad of bills and handed it to me. I said *Thank you,* and I tried to make it sound grateful but not fawning. He always overpaid me.

When the little boys tried to break down the bathroom door while I was inside, trying to shit into the ridiculous black toilet, I couldn't hold the door shut. The boys burst inside, giggling.

I didn't know that the parents of young children don't often keep the bathroom door shut. Little boys need to know where their mother is. I didn't know that, so when I finished shitting I spanked them. I was furiously ashamed.

Their mother kept hiring me, and I kept using the bathroom, and the little boys kept forcing their way in, and I kept spanking them. It never occurred to me to tell their mother.

One night, quite late, the little one came out of the bedroom, whimpering. He had a bloody nose. He'd had them before; I knew what to do. I pinched just below the bone and held it there, cooing comforting words, maybe singing a little song. He gagged on his blood.

I thought about how closely the two scenes had taken place: First, a spanking. Then, a comforting. I felt uncertain. Was I a spanker or a comforter?

I couldn't describe myself, couldn't choose. If I wasn't their mother, was I my mother?

———

I listened to music through headphones. I couldn't let my mother find out what I liked because she would jeer at me for liking something, and then she would take it away. But with the headphones, I was free. The music on my records, even though I couldn't buy them new, even though I had to scrounge used tapes and get my friends to tape over them, sent me outside the house, outside my life.

Even just hearing a television spot, late at night, for a two-album set of "guitar rock" as the song titles scrolled slowly by, I gained a small bit of vital fuel. What's curious to me now is that I didn't know at the time that I was suffering, so deeply involved was I in being saved.

I invented a shorthand notation for writing down bits of music that I heard on the radio, in a shop, or at the end of a movie. I remember sitting in the car, in the parking lot, having just seen a movie with my parents. My father was taking his time, using the bathroom, maybe, while my mother and I sat and waited. It was cold and dark in the car, and I was humming the music that had played over the end credits. I asked my mother if I could use her blue ballpoint pen and small spiral notebook that she wrote things in. *No!* she screamed. *Just be quiet!* Her bag was in her lap. It would have taken no effort at all.

Of that time, I remember just waiting for everyone and everything. I knew that even if I asked, no one would tell me why she was like that, so I just sat and waited for the day that I would never need to ride in a car with her again.

———

In eleventh grade I sat in the second row at a desk that seldom caught the eye of the geometry teacher, who was also the football coach. He had a patchy gray mustache and wore polo shirts tucked in over his belly. He seemed not to acknowledge the belly, and if you'd asked him if he had one, he'd have looked you right in the eye and denied it was there, and you'd believe him.

He didn't acknowledge the girls in the class, either, so I spent my time doodling on the putty-colored plastic desk. There was a horizontal groove along the top for a pencil. Otherwise it was smooth; no one had carved anything into it yet. I wrote a note on it in pencil—I don't remember what the first one said. *Hello. I am bored. Math is boring.*

A few days later I found writing on the desk in someone else's hand, under my note. *Hi! I also am bored. How are you doing? Are you real? Is the universe real? How can we know?*

Immediately I wanted to be in love with this bodiless, text-producing person. We had a secret. Between classes and during free periods I stuck my head inside the classroom. If it was empty, I ran in to read and write. One day, when I sat down, excitedly reading the new note—*I think I'm falling in love with you!*—Mr. Geometry dropped a pile of wet brown paper towels on the desk. I had to wipe my boyfriend clean away.

———

I checked the room for days until I knew who was writing to me. It was Wolf, a senior. He was the guitarist in a band, and everyone knew his name. I watched him read the desk. Some pretty girls leaned over the desk and read it, too, smiling and laughing into Wolf's face.

When he left the room with them, I walked past him and looked at his face and his blond hair. Then I stood in front of the desk and read it. I looked up to make sure he and the girls were still just outside the door. They were looking at me. Wolf looked neutral. The girls looked cruel. Then I looked back down and wrote on the desk, *I'm looking at you*.

Mr. Geometry skidded in and scolded me, but my heart was beating so fast for Wolf, I could have wrestled our teacher to the ground and punched him right in the belly, right in the mustache.

When I saw Wolf noodling on his guitar in the hallway one day, I walked up to him, for it was my destiny.

*Will you teach me how to play the guitar?* And then I stood there, waiting for him to say yes. He smiled and looked at me. He wasn't going to run away. I was talking to Wolf. An impossible thing was happening.

When I got home I asked my father if I could have a guitar, and he looked at me as if I should know better than to want something that we'd never even seen at a yard sale, but I understood. I wouldn't get a guitar, then or later, but I would be able to keep my imagined love with Wolf immaculate and perfect, all written out on the desk.

———

There was a tree-lined lake on the Emerson estate. One of the beaches was public. Bee and I rode our bikes to the lake and sat on the bank.

From the town's side, the Emersons' topiary garden looked like a gentle hill dotted with weird shrubs. We walked counterclockwise around the lake, picking our way through the pine forest full of sharp and slippery rocks, and climbed over two fences. The garden was a nearly vertical slope from which the sculpted trees grew perpendicular and then, a foot or two out of the ground, bent straight up. Even though the ground was soft, perfectly trimmed turf, it was hard not to fall down when you walked among the shaved and mutilated trees. Sometimes we were chased off the land, and sometimes we got to stay as long as we wanted.

We left our clothes on a dock and jumped in naked and bobbed there, two chatting heads on the gray water. We didn't have towels. While we were still in the water a group of girls from school appeared on the dock, as if they'd known to meet us. One of the girls on the deck had a towel, and the three of us used it. It wasn't good manners, but I wiped out my crack, front and back. God, that felt good, getting the lake water out of me. I thought I could somehow get dressed without anyone seeing my body, but of course my damp underwear twisted up my legs, and I had to stand there, hanging out, trying to get the underwear up and over me. I don't remember a thing about the other girls' bodies.

Bee and I went swimming together another time, and she left her swimsuit at my house afterward. It was a two-piece. My mother picked it up and examined the bra, checking the lining to see if there was any padding. *This has padding in it!* she screamed at me, furious because I wouldn't put on a two-piece swimsuit for all the money in the world. My mother was furious that I wouldn't make myself sexy for people to look at, to convince them that I was already grown up.

She and I brought a load of clothes to the dry cleaner, and the cashier said to me, wetly, right in front of my mother, *I like your body. It's slim and trim, like I like.* When we were back in the car, my mother looked at me and said, *Mmmm,* and smiled.

———

At the end of the year, I noticed Amber handing out party invitations printed on pale green paper. I could hear her talking to some other girls. Her brother Monroe was graduating from vocational school. My heart moved from my chest to my throat. It was hard to breathe. Even though Amber and I weren't really friends anymore, I knew at once that I would go to the party, and that in the throes of instability and betweenness, neither a high school student nor quite yet an adult, Monroe would become mine. I hadn't forgotten about Wolf, but the impending proximity to Monroe was much more exciting.

I went up to Amber and the group of girls, but the last two steps I took with great difficulty, as if there were a magnetic field pushing me away from them and back toward my quiet life. I asked Amber, *Are you having a party?* She looked at me blankly but not unkindly. Since I'd moved to Emerson Road, she and I no longer saw each other at the bus stop or in the neighborhood, and it had been a long time since we'd been in the same classes at school. I was getting good grades, collecting them like a miser, knowing that they would get me out of Waitsfield someday, and I knew that Amber had no such secret bounty, but she had something I didn't have: the capacity to be kind. She smiled and offered me a green sheet of paper. Monroe's party was on Saturday, at the Baptist church.

———

I sipped beer from a can. The beer bubbles were smaller than soda bubbles. They tasted like sour air.

The music was loud and the light was dim. All the high school seniors slouched against the concrete walls as if the room weren't big enough to take their whole, upright selves. Amber took my hand and we walked over to Monroe.

*You know Monroe is just my half brother, right?* she said, and then smiled wide at Monroe, the way he smiled at everyone. Amber's arms were stretched up to his shoulders, as at a school dance, but his massive arms held her as a father holds his prized daughter. Then she smiled at me. And then she turned back to him and they lined up their open mouths and pressed them together.

Then I went to the kitchen and poured myself a paper cup of punch and drank it right there, and then filled up my cup again and walked back out into the big room.

I scanned the room. Colleen Dooley was the only other girl from school I recognized. I went over to her. I had never been inside a church before, and I had never watched anyone my age kiss her brother before.

Colleen seemed ready to talk to me, as if she'd been waiting for me. She didn't even say hello. The first thing she said to me was that she was out of there if someone threw up. *Out of there.* She did not tolerate vomit. I knew that drinking a lot could make you vomit—my father occasionally came home drunk and then vomited so loudly that it sounded as if he were yelling—but everyone at the party was quiet, sipping, chatting, standing. No one was lurching, yelling, or falling down.

Then we heard a sound like water hitting the floor from a great height. Colleen got up and ran around a corner. I ran after her as if my life depended on it.

When we found an empty room, we crouched and shuddered. One by one the other girls from school drifted in. The last girl was exasperated. *You all run away and leave me, on my hands and knees, cleaning up!* As if this were a phase of any party; the chatting, the vomiting, the cleaning.

She was holding several of our coats. How did she know which one was mine? It was my mother's coat, a long brown felted wool. *This one . . .* she said. It had been hit with vomit. She had cleaned it. I took it and looked at it. I didn't see any vomit. There was a sour, bilious smell. No stains.

My father picked me up at eleven o'clock and I chewed a grainy piece of minty gum in the car on the way home.

The next night, or maybe the day after that, my mother asked, *Were people drinking at the party?—I guess so.—Were you drinking?* Before I could answer, my mother said, *He could smell it on your breath.*

## 16

In high school Charlie joined the tennis team and almost immediately started sleeping with the coach. Charlie's mother often chatted on the phone with me if I called when Charlie was at an imaginary tennis practice, having sex with the coach in his car, down by the brook. Her mother spoke to me as if I were real. I felt chosen.

One day Charlie's mother picked up the phone, and I said, *Hello, Prudence; this is Ruth.* Then I heard Prudence's voice at a short distance, as if she were holding the phone away from her but not covering the mouthpiece, as one would to speak privately, in those days.

She said, *It's Ruth, and I really don't want to talk with her right now.*

Then I heard Charlie's voice, greeting me as if nothing un-usual had happened. I said, *Your mother just said, "It's Ruth, and I really don't want to talk with her right now."* Charlie said, *No, she just said, "Charlie, it's Ruth on the phone."* I tried to reason with her.

Charlie despised the tennis coach for being in love with her. She told me that she'd stopped sleeping with the ten-nis coach long before she actually stopped, if she ever had stopped.

She referred to her big thighs as her *woman-legs*. She drove me to school in her own green Volvo. Her superstitions were many: she couldn't look at a digital clock if it showed the number thirteen; she wore only white underwear for years; she wore only black underwear for years; she couldn't walk past certain restaurants.

She had the loyalty of a three-year-old, loyalty without un-derstanding, the loyalty of the permanently terrified. The people she liked best were the ones who assured her of her absolute superiority.

Her favorite topic was what would become of people. To please her I would try to guess. Her leading questions al-ways skewed the answer toward conventional, and she would gasp at the dishonor of someone agreeing not to be extraordinary. Her worst fear was getting married and hav-ing children.

Her stepfather had so much money that she was able to live as if money didn't exist. It was just a bit of time between wanting and getting, the time it took to penetrate her tiny change purse with a finger and pull out a bill.

Before a party once she told me she had a white blouse and some black hose I could wear. The blouse was rank in the armpits, and the tights had a white crust.

She begged me to go to a party with her so she could seduce the captain of the tennis team. She had been drinking enough to be drunk or to pretend. She said, *Give me a kiss.*

I was afraid, so I kissed her cheek. I closed my eyes and inhaled.

*No, I want lips,* she said. My heart dissolved and I kissed her.

———

Back then, we'd been told that Officer Hill was an odd person. Sensitive. We thought that the tennis coach was odd, the volleyball coach was odd, Bee's father was odd, Amber's brother was a little odd, and it was particularly odd that one night, in ninth grade, Charlie had been picked up by a cop. She had been running through the field at school, screaming. And she was naked. Just screaming.

All of these Waitsfield girls together, with their burdens. Imagine twenty of them in a room, all day, thinking about each other. Thinking about what was still going to happen to them. They could see the future, a little. They so nobly faced it, patiently waiting.

All the girls in town thought they were unusual, that they were the only ones, the only weird, unlucky little ones. Some of them died of that bad luck, that terminal uniqueness. Some of them got pregnant and had babies and stopped being girls. And after that happened, those mothers took up the story they had been told, the big lie that had almost done them in, dusted it off and told it to their sons and daughters as if their lives depended on it. *That was just one time. It won't happen to you.*

In eleventh grade Colleen Dooley approached me sleepily in the hall one day, and told me that Amber and her mother had moved back to North Carolina. *I guess she'll have the baby down there,* she said. What baby? I wasn't surprised; I was confused, because a baby was impossible. Amber didn't go out with boys. Colleen suddenly glowed, superior, knowing. How did she always find things out first?

*Monroe was only her half brother,* she said, and then stared at me as if she wanted to memorize everything I said or did in that moment, the moment that I learned Monroe and Amber were going to be the parents of a baby together, finally all grown up and far from Waitsfield, where such a thing could never have happened.

———

In those days Charlie went out and got drunk several nights a week, and whenever I saw her the following day she would look at me bashfully. *Charlie, did it happen again?—Yeah, I think it happened again,* she'd say.

Charlie had said that she liked to keep the tennis coach inside her for as long as possible afterward so that she could still feel him. Sometime after that, she said that he had broken a few of her ribs while on a bender. After that, she said that the story of the broken ribs had been a lie. After that, she said she'd thought it was a lie but once she told it, she'd realized it was the truth.

I don't know whether she ever really slept with the tennis coach, or with anyone.

Charlie's stepfather disappeared one day with his secretary and quickly disinherited the children, who took their mother's name, the better name, after all was said and done.

Toward the end of the year, Charlie said to me, *What do you think people would do if I didn't show up for school tomorrow?* and I said that if she was going to cut class, it wasn't worth it, that she should just sit through the last few days of school before the year was over. We were no longer in class with the odious Ryan O'Reilly, who had been put into remedial courses. At the end of class, Charlie raised her hand and said, *Madame? Je suis désolée, mais je ne peux pas participer à la classe demain,* and Madame made a mark in her attendance book, and that was the last time I ever saw Charlie.

I brought my lunch to school and ate alone, in one of the classrooms in the English wing. Sometimes I wasn't alone; some other sad sacks found the same dark room and picked different corners. One afternoon I walked into the classroom of the teacher who advised the school newspaper. Colleen Dooley was already there, lunch in hand. She stood in front of the teacher's desk while he sat on it as if riding sidesaddle, casual and handsome. She spoke, as always, in her annoying newscaster voice, insipid and fraught. In one breath she said that Charlie had committed suicide and in the next breath, looking under a slice of bread, said, *Ugh, I just hate my sandwich today.*

The teacher could see that the news had wrapped around me, smothering me. I couldn't accept that it was true, but I knew that someone as stupid as Colleen Dooley wouldn't make up such a story. The teacher got her to leave. Then he told me that I would never forget Charlie, and that I should write a letter to her parents, telling them that she had been my friend, and that I wouldn't ever forget her. Then he let me sit in his empty room for as long as I wanted.

He was a lazy teacher, but he had a reserve of energy that allowed him to rise to that occasion. He never seemed completely like a teacher, I think, because he didn't see us as his dumb audience. So it seemed as if he weren't teaching, hadn't prepared any silly little educational tunes like the ones the other teachers intoned. They all sounded like Colleen. They all just wanted to put on a show of being teachers. Colleen was stupid, but she was smart enough to know that being a newscaster, singing her newsy song into the silent, soulless lens, was the perfect job for someone like her.

I wrote Charlie's parents a letter, but they didn't respond. Time passed. I didn't hear about a funeral.

The weekly *Courier* always ran a human-interest story on the front page, above the fold. A photo of a squirrel in a fountain, or children playing near a fire truck or holding ice cream cones. Turn a few pages, and the wedding, birth, and death announcements followed. The police blotter was always the same: a little light trespassing and vandalism, traffic stops, and domestic calls. Charlie's obituary never ran.

*If you find out how she did it, tell me,* said a sad boy, looking at me intently. *I will,* I said, feeling numb, but I never found out, and I wouldn't have told him if I had.

I never asked and never found out, but I knew that she had been waiting for it to happen, as if it had come from somewhere outside herself. I think it did. She died by her own hand, but she was as brave as a soldier before a firing squad. She faced it. Whatever it was, she had been facing it for a long time.

## 17

*What should I wear?* my mother wailed. She tried on several outfits. Her cousins were driving in from New York for Aunt Rose's funeral. I'd never met them. It was thrilling to know that finally we would meet each other on equal footing.

Sitting at the service, my head facing forward and slightly down, I looked around with my eyes. I wondered who was who. We sat under a canopy on plastic folding chairs. My cousin Dvora led the service. I had never met her before. Her voice sounded confident and calm.

When Dvora asked if anyone wanted to say a few words, she looked at me kindly, and my throat closed, and I had to shake my head without saying anything. And then I cried. I hated crying in front of my parents. Crying felt like something that animals did, something that strong people didn't need to do. I knew that I was weak. I had trouble driving in traffic, couldn't navigate rotaries, never knew when I had the right-of-way to turn left. I always assumed the other cars would cut me off or try to hit me as I trembled in my mother's car, flinching at intersections, weeping and sweating.

———

After Aunt Rose's funeral there was a luncheon for her remaining siblings and their children and grandchildren. Everyone was introduced. Uncle Roger the widower was there, and so were his two children. His son, Bobby, lived in New York, and his daughter, Debbie, lived in Chicago. Bobby was cosmopolitan and had a daughter, Brett, in elementary school, and a tall and elegant wife. Debbie was frumpy and her daughter, Dvora, was in her twenties.

Uncle Roger's eyes were small and black, and his dyed black hair looked shellacked. His eyebrows were thin and black and had sharp peaks. He looked important and pleased and cruel. I sat between Dvora and my mother; Dvora sat between me and hers.

As we ate buttered bread my cousin and I asked each other polite questions. When we had learned a bit about each other, we sat quietly and ate olives and drank ice water. Then, after we had been quiet for a short time, she leaned her head close to mine and said that Uncle Roger had raped

Debbie, her mother, for fourteen years, starting when she was two.

At the other end of the table Uncle Roger tickled Brett, his fingers in her ear like a lover's. Wrapping her hair around his fingers, kissing her neck, whispering in her ear. She beamed. She was eight or nine years old, in hair ribbons.

I sat perfectly still. My mouth was dry and I wasn't sure I could swallow the bread in my mouth. Dvora said, *So now you know something about this family.*

I looked at Bobby, who was smiling into the air, carefully ignoring his father. Uncle Roger and Brett sat nearby with their heads touching.

The little girl's mother got up and left the table. Bobby explained to us that she had papers to grade. She was a teacher. She would have to go to the car and grade papers, there were so many. He smiled so widely that his little eyes squinted almost shut.

There were plenty of things on my plate to eat. I used the knife and fork with great care, tasted the food and chewed it all up.

The mother came back after a while and sat back down. Then she got up again and left for a long time. I couldn't believe what Uncle Roger was doing to his granddaughter.

We drove home and I changed back into regular clothes and sat down on the sofa to read. As soon as I opened my book, the phone rang and I picked it up on the second ring and said hello. *This is Vera Goldberg.* It was my mother's aunt Vera, Uncle Irving's widow.

My mother's paternal uncle Irving was the first person I ever knew who died. He had lived in an apartment with his wife, Vera, and had a whole room for his model trains. Vera collected dolls and displayed them in the living room on shelves. One shelf held framed black-and-white photographs of children sitting in rows and wearing old-fashioned home-sewn clothes, for Aunt Vera and Uncle Irving had grown up in Boston together. They had no children and lived together for decades before getting married. Uncle Irving's vice was cherry soda, and Aunt Vera's was cigarettes. She had a movie star's sultry voice.

The last time I'd seen Vera, Uncle Irving had just died of diabetes, and my mother and I had made our first and only condolence call. Vera had sat in a chair, perpendicular to us, looking straight ahead, while my mother told Vera all the things that she and I had done that week. Vera seemed to vibrate with a pain that my mother didn't acknowledge. Occasionally Vera said something about Irving to which my mother made no response. Vera was so angry, she seemed to shrivel. My mother and I sat there, in that apartment of grief, held and protected by our separate reality.

On the phone Vera sounded both shrill and hoarse, as if she'd just been shouting or crying. She spoke fast, as if she'd practiced. *I am sorry for your loss but I wanted you to know that I think that you are very cold, cold people!*

I said *I know,* but she had already hung up.

After Rose died, Roger lived a few more years. In his *Courier* obituary he was lauded for having been *larger than life, with a prodigious temper, but the flip side of it was his enormous passion for mentoring young playwrights.* Prodigious temper. Enormous passion. Young playwrights. The tennis coach. Officer Hill. Monroe. And Bee's father, who was now a grandfather.

Years later, riding the D line home from seeing a movie in Boston by myself, all the way from Park Street in the center of Boston to the suburban stop where I'd parked my father's car, I felt a rubbing sensation against the back of my puffy coat. The skinny train car was packed, and we were all hanging on to straps or seats, swaying in time to the train's rocking. A woman a few feet away caught my eye and stared into my face with an intensity that had to mean something, but what? Was she flirting with me? Was someone robbing me? No, my bag was hanging in front of me and I had zipped it shut. My mother's warning, that thieves carried scissors to cut the leather straps of bags from women's shoulders, was insane. The woman kept staring at me, relentless.

A lot of people got out of the train at the commuter hub, but I still had five stops to go. The woman carefully moved herself down the car, shifting her hands from strap to seat to strap, until she was standing right in front of me. *He was masturbating!* she stage-whispered. The rubbing I'd felt and immediately thrust from my head because it was too creepy to consider was a man masturbating against my anorak-insulated body. I never saw the guy, but I had a sense of him. He reminded me of Bee's father.

———

I graduated from high school and kept babysitting and working at a bookstore, collecting money for some yet unimagined future.

When I'd graduated from high school, my mother had given me a pair of diamond earrings she didn't want anymore, and when she saw them one day, just lying on my plastic makeup tray, she took them back, saying that I hadn't taken good care of them, and I understood that they'd never been mine at all; they were just a placeholder for a gift she was expected to give, and that after she'd fulfilled that contract, she'd dissolved it when no one was looking. She'd often said that when she died I'd have all her jewelry. I'd liked looking at her opal ring and told her so. She'd said it was bad luck to wear an opal if it wasn't your birthstone. At some point I asked to see it again and she said that she had sold it.

I learned to knit from a library book and knitted a scarf with high-gauge needles, in thick pink and orange yarn, with a knotted-on fringe, and gave it to my mother. My mother borrowed my knitting needles and the remains of the yarn, and she knitted the same scarf, half pink and half orange, with the same fringe. Her stitches were more regular than mine. She wore hers and gave the one I'd made back to me.

My mother got angry at me more often than before, and now that I was out of high school, she said, I should be paying rent. Her father had collected rent from her until she was married and moved in with my father, she said. She never specified an amount, though, and I sensed that she didn't want to collect the rent as much as she wanted me to feel as if I owed it to her.

One afternoon she and I were folding a stack of fresh towels. They smelled like fake flowers.

*When I got my first period,* my mother softly said, *that's when my father stopped spanking me.*

She looked at me. In that moment she didn't look imperious. She looked tired and sad, as if she wanted to take good care of me but knew that she couldn't, that no one could protect a child from being hurt, that no one could take care of anyone. What had happened to her was too horrible to say, so she never said it.

Then I knew what she had been trying to do. My mother had borne my loathing for years like someone wrongly accused, quietly serving her unearned sentence, knowing that one day she would be free, but not yet. If I wore a padded two-piece swimsuit, no bad man would touch me; I would already be grown up, impervious to harm. I would move far away and be safe. I would outlive her father. I would outlive my father. And, one day, I would outlive her.

The kitchen radio was playing light static and an old man's voice. My mother was emitting energy, moving around, wiping at the front of the cabinets with the dish sponge. She used that sponge to wipe the floor sometimes if it was just a tiny spill. The counters. The table. She punished that sponge until it was gray.

I knew all my mother's stories by heart and loved to ask her what she remembered, to see if any new details crept in. In kindergarten there was a tray of cookies that fell on the floor, and no one admitted to having knocked it over, so my mother and another girl both had to stay after school. In junior high there was a fat girl whom everyone on the school bus called Tubbins. In high school there was a girl who danced in a nightclub. *She had boobs the size of this room,* my mother said.

Now I wanted to ask her about the new story. I started asking it while I was looking at my mother, but by the end of it

I had to look away. I had never asked my mother this question before.

*What did he do to you?*

Her face was slack. She looked like a girl who doesn't yet know what she looks like. Like someone who eats lunch alone in an empty house and doesn't recognize that her table manners have deteriorated. *What?* she said. As if she had no idea what I was asking.

*What did he do?* I repeated. I needed to know so I could start building a container for that information, to keep it safe, so it wouldn't join the rest of my memories and contaminate them. I needed to keep it separate, accessible but protected.

She didn't say anything. I heard the radio, and I watched my mother's arms moving against the kitchen counter and the sink. Then she looked at me, and I knew she would punish me for making it real.

I was standing in one doorway, and then she was walking out of the room. I followed her to the living room, where the vacuum had left perfect parallel lines in the synthetic rug. Normally I wasn't allowed to walk on them.

She walked over to the low table and got down on her knees and brushed invisible bits of dust from it. She readjusted the two bowls of pine cones. Then she pushed herself up with her big arms and hands and thick pink-brown nails. *I am your mother!* she said. That was all she said, and I finally understood why she didn't recognize herself as a ruined person. It was clear to me that what had happened to her wasn't rare but normal, that it was too common even to register as a story. It wasn't even a story at all.

All the Waitsfield girls, in their little rooms, all through the town, lie down and wait and breathe. Their scalps sweat into their pillows. Their hearts slow down as they drift off. The girls are walking to school. The sides of their noses itch. They scratch them and collect flakes of dead skin under their nails. They are keeping secrets. They feel special because they have been told that they are. Each of them, one in a million.

If they ever tell anyone what happened to them, they will all be told the same thing: that it won't happen again. Even if it keeps happening, every time, they will be told that it will never happen again, over and over. Once in a lifetime, over and over.

18

It occurred to me that there was a third way, besides dying or getting pregnant, for a girl to get out of Waitsfield. You could go crazy, by which I mean you could agree to be the person whom everyone else in town would bring up, for the rest of their lives, as a tragic example.

I'd wanted to die, or for my mother to die, or for us both to die, for years. Now I was finally ready to say it out loud.

She and my father drove me to the hospital, and I calmly answered all of the intake questions. When the triage nurse asked me if I thought things would ever improve, I said no, because I knew they wouldn't. She rewarded me for that answer with a cold hamburger and admittance to the psychiatric ward. I said goodbye to my parents, got into a wheelchair, and rode up to the ninth floor. I gave my knapsack to the nurses' station to be searched. I was led to a room full of sleeping women, and I got into the one empty cot and slept. In the morning, someone came in to wake us up, and I got out of bed. The other women stayed asleep.

———

Dr. Specter's hair was shoe-polish black, and her skin was yellowish under the dirty ceiling lights. She accused me of trying to fool her into giving me medicine, but I didn't want any medicine. I just wanted to stop feeling.

Dr. Specter was at least twenty years older than I was. I stared into her eyeholes.

Dr. Specter had come to Waitsfield on purpose. She had chosen to practice psychiatry in a small county hospital. She writhed in her chair. She'd spent more than a decade earning degrees so that she could end up in an institution for the powerless, where she could finally be in charge.

*You're being weak. You need to show some character,* she said. My first thought was that she'd gotten it wrong; I was there because I had used up all my strength, and that no one should be expected to continue as I'd been. But that was the treatment she had to offer. She thought I needed more cruelty, that I had a deficiency of that vitamin. To my surprise I began weeping. I didn't even try to hide or wipe my face. *Get your act together!* she said. Maybe it worked on some people.

Until then I'd thought that the hospital, that playground for sadists, was actually a place where sick people got better.

The trash cans on the ward held paper sacks instead of plastic liners. Plastic bags fell into the category of *sharps,* even if they weren't sharp. The laundry soap was powdered. There were no tools to get the chain off the exercise bike. Windows were double-sealed. The shower curtain rod was hollow.

My favorite therapy-mate was Carl the schizophrenic, the only chronic on the ward. He'd been on Haldol for more than twenty years. Sometimes he stood, dazed, in the common room, holding a chair above his head, but he gently put it down if anyone mentioned it.

Next to the nurses' station was a sign-out board. The alcoholics all got to sign out every day for EKGs of their weakened hearts, and those who received electroconvulsive therapy signed out in the morning and were signed back in when they were brought back upstairs, unconscious, on stretchers.

Carl was the only one on the ward who wasn't allowed out for any reason. On his nineteenth day without outdoor privileges, he signed PATIENT: *Carl*; DESTINATION: *Aruba*; TIME OUT: *2001.* He got in trouble.

———

For attending all of my therapy groups with Dr. Specter for a week, I earned a weekend furlough.

A therapist unlocked the combination lock on the ward door and led me into the elevator and into the lobby and out the hospital door and into the parking lot. People stood around and sucked on cigarettes, their shoulders hunched against the cold.

My father appeared in the car and I got in and we drove home without speaking.

While I was home I didn't take the antipsychotics that put me to sleep and I got the shakes and didn't eat anything in a day and a half and then, since I felt unreal, I said something that someone would say in a different family: *I need your support.* My mother just looked at me and said, *Vomit.*

My father drove me back on the morning of the second day. I was crying hard and still shaking. I didn't want to go back.

I remember pushing people away from me if they got close enough that I could see the lines in their faces, and someone said the word *restraints* and then wrapped my wrists in something soft that attached to the sides of the metal bed frame, and then they injected me with something in the crook of my elbow, and then my nose itched and my ears itched on the insides and my chin itched just under my lip and I scraped my front teeth along that itch, but I couldn't move my hands more than an inch out from the sides of the bed, and that's how they left me.

———

When I woke up I was in a room that was bigger and quieter. My feet were pointing toward the door, which was off to the left. I couldn't tell how far away it was, or how far away the walls were. The room seemed enormous. It seemed to throb outward, breathing, getting bigger and bigger, like a girl getting ready to scream.

One of the warders came by every half hour, saying *Checks . . . checks . . . checks . . .* quietly as he approached my half-open door, so he wouldn't scare me. He was checking to make sure I was still there and not dead. I felt called to, like an animal in a barnyard. I liked anticipating the next check. It always came.

———

Years and years ago, the elementary school psychologist had sat us in a circle and asked us to name the colors that matched our feelings. I don't remember what I said, but I remember that the psychologist went last and closed his smug little eyes for a moment as he told us that he felt *TEE-ull, which is a sort of greenish blue.*

Each year, the psychologist returned and put us in a circle again. We went around saying our colors, and I hated him and said that I was an ugly orange. He went last again, of course, and said that today he felt *like TEE-ull, which is a sort of greenish blue.*

I'd have raised my hand and called him out on his counterfeit feeling, but he was just like Officer Hill, and he was the same as the visiting speaker who ended his presentation by misquoting the last line from a popular movie on purpose, as if we wouldn't notice. These men thought we were stupid. They couldn't imagine what to say to us unless they were teaching us something. We were inert targets at which to aim their certainty, and even if we knew they were wrong, the men couldn't even imagine not being right. So many of them would never know what was actually true. And that's the secret, useless power we had over them.

When the nurses and the social workers and the medical students checked on us, they always said *checks,* so when I heard a real knock on the door, I knew it wasn't a staff member. I said *Come in.*

The door opened, and standing there was the enormous man who dressed like a child dressed as an old-timey grandpa. He lived with his mother, but he wanted to move to a group home, so his mother had sent him here for a tune-up. He must have been at least fifty years old, but he had a goal. And now had a mission.

*I'm going around to all the rooms,* he said in his gentle voice, as if a loud noise would trigger a rock slide. He shuffled his feet in the doorway a little and I realized that he was a hero, now that he was moving out of his mother's house. Now that he could do anything, he was going to be a person who took care of people. Suddenly I could see that he was a soldier, just standing there in the doorway, his delicate white wrists hanging out of his worn shirtsleeves. He looked the way I felt on the day I spoke to Wolf, after weeks of confessing all my unrequited desires in pencil, on my desk, in geometry class.

*Are you scared; do you need anything,* he said. Of course I wasn't scared; I wasn't insane. And, unlike him, I hadn't lived in my mother's house for fifty years. I hadn't even lived there for twenty-five years, and though I didn't have a plan, I was pretty sure that I'd get out before I was fifty. But just in case I didn't, I made sure to properly appreciate him. Thank you, brave warrior. Thank you for rescuing me in the dark.

———

I had already waited as long as I could, calculating how long it would take for someone to untie me. And someone did come in, two someones, a woman and a man, but instead of untying me from the bed they yanked my pants down and shoved a bowl under my ass, and just as quickly walked out of the room. The edges of the bowl pressed into me painfully. My ass pressed against the bottom of the bowl.

I pissed a hot gin-clear fury and moaned with the relief of it. I closed my eyes while my poison piss killed a field of nightmare poppies, not caring where it went, when someone slipped through the partly closed door. Most of my attention was on my relief, but I could see that it was a doctor.

He was short and had a round face. His mouth made an O! in a mockery of surprise, as if he'd wandered in by accident.

Dr. X stood and watched. He watched me, but I didn't care because I wasn't in my body anymore. Let him look at it doing its things, lying there in the bed. Mentally, I was years in the future, imagining an actual life.

He stood at some distance from the bed, and then when he came to me, his face mirrored the relief I felt, sitting in my bed-toilet. He didn't say anything but I thought of him as having come in while under control of a force he wasn't exactly in charge of. He looked helpless, and I guess, in a way, he was.

He yanked on himself a few times at an exploratory velocity and then violently and fast and then I felt something on my thighs. It felt warm. Some of it slid down into the bowl. My wrists were still tied to the bed.

A moment afterward, a nurse came in and saw him standing over a girl tied to her bed rails. The nurse took the bowl away and the bed was still wet under me, and she gave me another shot in the crook of my elbow and my eyes stopped seeing.

———

The day I was released from the hospital, two therapists woke me in the morning. I don't know what time it was. I used the toilet and washed my hands and face in the cold-water drip. No soap. They let me sit on the side of the bed and feed myself breakfast with a bent metal spoon from an unbreakable plastic bowl. I was hungry. I asked for more food, and they took my bowl and spoon away. To my surprise they brought a second bowl, and there was a sliced banana in it. I ate it all, even the brown bits.

Then I left my room and went to sit in the common room for the morning group meeting. When it was my turn to speak I said that my three goals for the day were getting dressed, going home, and never coming back.

I took a shower and looked at the line of old shampoos and soaps that people had left behind. When I was done I carefully wiped off my own bottles and brought them back to my room. Then I got dressed. When I was called to the front desk, my father was standing there. *Hi, Ruthie,* he said. He looked old.

The desk nurse was inside the glass-doored, double-locked sharps closet behind the front desk. She fished out my portable cassette player and tapes, my hair dryer, my little tube of hydrocortisone cream, my tweezers, razor, nail clipper, and vitamin pills. All the things they had ruled too dangerous for me to keep.

Then, after signing some papers, I walked out of there, carrying a secret, the secret of the minotaur, Dr. X, who shall remain in his maze, nameless and faceless.

———

I waited a few months, and then I went to the bank and got a cashier's check made out to my mother. On the memo line I wrote *17 Emerson Road*. I kept enough bookstore and babysitting money in my account to cover three months of rent in an apartment share with Colleen Dooley, who had moved out west, across the state line, to New York. I don't know how much of Winifred's house had been left to pay off, but it didn't matter. I had paid what I could. A contract had been executed.

On the way home from the bank, I walked through the Congregational churchyard. *Patience,* one of my favorite gravestones read. That's all it said. It was a baby's grave. Impatient little thing! She got out of Waitsfield before almost anyone.

I'd like to say that I never went back to town after I moved away, but I went back for the holidays, and the bus ride was eighty-four dollars, round trip, because I hadn't moved very far away at all. The roadside snowbanks were higher because the roads were better plowed, and they were darker gray, almost black, because there was more traffic. Riding the bus back to Waitsfield took four hours, enough time to get ready to change from one person back to another.

I still went with my parents to their favorite diner, where the owner described my appearance to my mother as if he were selling me to her.

My father never touched me, and maybe that was the improvement on her own childhood that my mother had been satisfied with. Her father had hurt her, and maybe Uncle Roger had, too. She never said. It wasn't her fault that they had rendered her inhuman, but I still had to get away. Otherwise I'd never stop hating her, and then I wouldn't have been any better than anyone else in that shit-frozen town.

My life didn't feel as if it had a wound, or a missing piece, or any of the metaphors we used in group therapy with Dr. Specter. None of those metaphors matched my feeling. It wasn't even a feeling. It just felt like *waiting*.

Decades passed, and then one day, some years into raising a child of my own—who has grown up knowing ordinary love and whose life is unremarkable—without even trying, without any expectation, without even really noticing what had happened, I saw that I'd stopped waiting.

# Acknowledgments

I owe profoundest thanks to PJ Mark, who bore the standard into the fire; to Parisa Ebrahimi, who edited this book brilliantly and tirelessly; and to my beloved son, Sam Chapman, who kept me anchored to the actual earth. I also wish to thank my early readers, Ian Bonaparte, Meghan Cleary, Amy Fusselman, Sheila Heti, Philip Gwyn Jones, Elizabeth McCracken, Maile Meloy, Ethan Nosowsky, Julie Orringer, Ed Park, Zadie Smith, and Antoine Wilson; and for research assistance I wish to thank Dylan Boyd, Emily Herzog, Jess Jonas, and Ted Mulkerin. I reserve my utmost gratitude for Diane Kramer, the oracle.

SARAH MANGUSO is the author of seven previous books, including *300 Arguments, Ongoingness, The Guardians,* and *The Two Kinds of Decay.* Honors for her writing include a Guggenheim Fellowship and the Rome Prize. She grew up in Massachusetts and now lives in Los Angeles. *Very Cold People* is her first novel.

sarahmanguso.com

## About the Type

This book was set in Fairfield, the first typeface from the hand of the distinguished American artist and engraver Rudolph Ruzicka (1883–1978). Ruzicka was born in Bohemia (in the present-day Czech Republic) and came to America in 1894. He set up his own shop, devoted to wood engraving and printing, in New York in 1913 after a varied career working as a wood engraver, in photoengraving and banknote printing plants, and as an art director and freelance artist. He designed and illustrated many books, and was the creator of a considerable list of individual prints—wood engravings, line engravings on copper, and aquatints.